Praise for *Breathing on Her Own*

"Lean, not florid, genuine, not sappy, reflective, not preachy, familiar, not clichéd, satisfying, not contrived: what more could one ask of a contemporary novel from a first-time novelist? Readers of *Breathing on Her Own* will enjoy a story that feels close to home, in the tradition of writers like Anne Tyler. We know the people in this story. They are friends, neighbors, family, even ourselves. I expect that when readers finish this book, they will ask Dr. Waters when they can read her next one. That's certainly my question."

—JON WEATHERLY
Vice President for Academic Affairs/Provost Johnson University

"Entertaining, challenging, and realistic. *Breathing on Her Own* brings us face-to-face with what we really believe through the eyes of one woman's journey with hope and resilient faith as the backbone of the story."

—DREW WATERS
Actor, Director, Producer; Star of *The Ultimate Life* and *The Redemption of Henry Meyers* as well as recurring roles on *Saturday Night Lights* and *NCIS*

"I was hooked from the beginning! Waters takes us on a journey of faith and doubt which had me asking questions like, 'How would I react?' and 'Would I trust God during these tough times?' Let this real-life drama pull you in and pull you closer to God!"

—ANDY LYNCH
WTLW TV host of 'Faith and Friends' and Sports Director of WOSN

"Rebecca Waters nailed it in this well-written novel about family and life changing tragedy. She takes her protagonist, Molly, through the pain that comes when life kicks you in the gut, in both a realistic and insightful way. Giving Molly permission to question her God and her faith gives the reader permission to do the same. This can bring a great deal of comfort to people who are struggling through the challenges that inevitably come into every life. In *Breathing on Her Own*, as in real life, God holds up to the questioning and that is the message that Ms. Waters handles so well."

—ROBIN PRINCE MONROE

Author of *Devotions for the Brokenhearted* and the *Comforting Little Hearts* series

"A must read. Edge of your seat drama, *Breathing on Her Own* is as brilliant as it is captivating. Rebecca Waters has the ability to paint an accurate picture of her delightful characters in this poignant yet heart warming story that deals with real life issues."

—R. A. GIGGIE

Author of *Stella's Plea*

Breathing
-ON HER-
own

Rebecca Waters

Ambassador International
GREENVILLE, SOUTH CAROLINA & BELFAST, NORTHERN IRELAND

www.ambassador-international.com

Breathing on Her Own

ISBN: 978-1-62020-733-8
eISBN: 978-1-62020-753-6
Library of Congress Control Number: 2019952197

This is a work of fiction. Names, characters, and incidents are all products of the author's imagination or are used for fictional purposes. Any mentioned brand names, places, and trademarks remain the property of their respective owners, bear no association with the author or the publisher, and are used for fictional purposes only.

Scripture quotations are taken from the HOLY BIBLE NEW INTERNATIONAL VERSION® NIV® Copyright© 1973, 1978, 1984 by International Bible Society. Used by permission of Zondervan Publishing House. All rights reserved.

Cover Design and Page Layout by Hannah Nichols

AMBASSADOR INTERNATIONAL
Emerald House
411 University Ridge, Suite B14
Greenville, SC 29601, USA
www.ambassador-international.com

AMBASSADOR BOOKS
The Mount
2 Woodstock Link
Belfast, BT6 8DD, Northern Ireland, UK
www.ambassadormedia.co.uk

The colophon is a trademark of Ambassador, a Christian publishing company.

For my mother, who shared three precious gifts with me:
Life, a love for the Lord, and a love for books.

Acknowledgments

Asking a new author to acknowledge those who helped in bringing a project to fruition is a bit like asking a first-time Academy Award winner to offer a "brief speech."

Without a doubt, God tops the list. God gave me the desire to write, the story to tell, the words to use, and the people to contact.

One of those contacts is Bethany Kaczmarek who worked with me to polish and perfect my work. Thank you, Bethany for your support, continued interest, and patience in teaching me to be a better writer. I want to thank Ambassador International who has recognized the worth of this work. Sam Lowry's confidence in me as an author is true encouragement. The team at Ambassador International is so very good. A special thank you to Hannah Nichols who nailed the cover design.

Thank you, David Hargrave, for allowing me to use bits and pieces of your wonderful sermons in this work. And my appreciation to my dear friends, Charlie and Susan, who serve as role models for facing tough issues with strength and faith.

I must also mention the immense support of friends and colleagues who have prayed me through the process and agreed to help me get the word out as soon as the book is published. The people who read my blog and offer words of encouragement or share something

I've written. Those small pieces offer incredible support. People like Nancy and Marty, and Tammie and Jon, Evelyn and Mark, and Beth, Kevin, Susan, Natalie, and Lorie. Others, like Sharon, Leah, and Brenda. The list goes on.

But I still could not have completed this journey without my family. My husband, Tom, called me a writer before I called myself one. He cooked dinners for me when I was in the throes of revision and read my story from page one—over and over as it went through multiple changes. My sweet husband died tragically in a bicycle accident only months after the first release of *Breathing on Her Own*. I know him. He would celebrate this second opportunity to bring this story to a new audience.

My daughters, Allison, Danielle, and Kendall, along with their husbands and children, have encouraged me through this endeavor. They laugh and tease each other, suggesting I have taken one or more attributes from my own children to develop my characters. They're only half-right. I did use some of the good parts.

Tom and the girls were first readers for my work. I've counted on them to give me feedback. They didn't hesitate. I like that about my family.

And there's my mother, Nora. Thank you, Mom, for the confidence you have in me and the confidence you have instilled in me.

I now realize there may be one name on the front cover, but an army behind each and every writer.

I may watch the Academy Awards with a new appreciation this year.

Chapter 1

MOLLY TIPTON FOLLOWED HER HUSBAND through the wide glass doors of the emergency room to the nurse's station. A male nurse on the telephone at a desk at the back of the cubicle didn't look up. Molly's heart pounded. She brought her hand down hard on the bell in front of her.

"We were told our daughter Laney was in an accident and brought here." Travis' voice sounded steady, but Molly saw his lower lip twitch. "Laney Tipton."

"Camden. Alana Camden," Molly corrected. Laney and Rob had been married for over ten years, but Laney would always be Travis' little girl. At least to him.

"That's right. Camden." Travis rubbed his forehead as he turned to Molly. "How often have I done that?"

The nurse, whose nametag read "Howard," typed the information into the computer. "That's Camden with a 'C'? Here we go." Howard looked up. "Her husband is with her. If you'll take a seat, I'll check on her status." Nurse Howard motioned to the plastic chairs lining the waiting room walls. He sounded calm. Maybe Laney was okay. Rob was with her. Travis guided her to the seating area as Howard disappeared through a security door leading to the examination rooms.

Molly reached into her purse for her cell phone. "Should I call Lissa?"

"Let's wait. It's almost two in the morning. There's nothing she can do, and we don't even know exactly what happened." Travis the practical. Travis the analytical. Travis the wise. Molly put her phone away. A moment later, the security door opened, and Rob emerged, weary and bent. Molly and Travis leaped to their feet to meet him.

"How is she?"

"What happened?"

Rob pulled his mouth tight. "They're taking her to surgery right now."

"Surgery? What kind of surgery?"

"They have to stop some internal bleeding." Rob's eyes began to tear up. "She doesn't look good."

Molly's heart quickened. She forced herself to breathe. "Where are the kids?"

"At home in bed. My sister came over."

"What happened, Rob?" Travis put his hand on the younger man's back.

"You know Old Creek Road? Where the hill comes down, and you have to make that sharp left turn? I guess she didn't make the turn and slid off the road." It was a dangerous road. Only last fall, a truck carrying milk from the local dairy farms had flipped over at the turn, killing the driver.

"I bet it was icy," Travis said.

"What was she doing on Old Creek Road?" Molly asked. "That's clear on the other side of town."

"I don't know. Laney called around eleven and said they were leaving River Rats. She was driving Tori back to where she was staying and said I should go on to bed." Rob drew in a deep breath. "The next thing I knew, the police were pounding on my door."

Tori! Laney said she was meeting friends after work. Molly had picked up the children after school and kept them for the two hours before Rob came home. But she didn't know the plans had included Tori Johnson. She hadn't even known Laney's college friend was in town.

Tori was like a female version of Eddie Haskell from *Leave it to Beaver*. *"Oh, yes, Mrs. Tipton, I believe that our primary concern our first year of college should be to focus on our studies."*

The first time she'd picked up Laney for a long weekend home, Laney hefted a full laundry bag into the back seat, most of which proved to be the large, shaggy rug from her room. "What happened to your rug?" she had asked.

"Tori Johnson happened. She threw up all over it."

"I hope she's not contagious."

"She didn't have the flu, Mom. She was drunk. She just walked into our room and puked all over my rug. She's gross."

Over the course of their freshman year, Laney's attitude toward Tori had changed. Molly attributed it to Andrea, Laney's roommate. Tori was like the Pied Piper, pulling Andrea and Laney to do her bidding.

"I think she just needed that first year to grow up," Laney said.

Grow up indeed! It was just like Tori to talk Laney into driving her out to wherever she was staying without consideration for how far out of the way it would be. Or that Laney had a loving husband and two beautiful children waiting for her at home. Or that Laney would have to navigate unfamiliar country roads late at night with snow and ice everywhere. No, Tori hadn't grown up at all. She was still the same selfish girl she had been in college. This was all Tori's fault. Tori was the reason Molly's precious daughter was lying on some cold surgical table having who-knows-what done to her. A shiver went up Molly's spine. She hugged her arms around herself just as Howard reentered the room.

"Mr. Camden? You and your family can come with me upstairs. There's a private waiting room outside the surgical suite."

Molly and Travis followed Rob and Nurse Howard to the fourth floor. The room was small but more comfortably appointed with two soft, brown chairs and a loveseat. A crucifix hung on the wall opposite the door, reminding Molly they were in a Catholic hospital. It also reminded her of what her friend Marianne called the power of prayer. Molly sat down on one of the brown chairs and shoved her face into her hands.

"You okay?" Travis asked.

"Just praying," Molly whispered.

For the first twenty minutes, Travis flipped through a magazine. Then, he investigated the coffee pot in the corner.

"This stuff is like mud. I'm going to find us some fresh coffee, Molly. Rob, can I get you anything?"

Rob shook his head.

Molly got up to check out the pot. The liquid in the pot was dark, old, and burnt, evidence of a vigil held in this very room just hours earlier. She dumped the remains in the small, stainless sink and began rinsing the glass carafe.

"Rob," Molly asked tentatively as she searched the cabinet for a paper towel, "if they went out to eat, what were they doing at River Rats? I mean, isn't that a bar?"

"They were going clubbing. You know, dancing and stuff."

That didn't bother you? Molly bit her lip to keep from asking, but Rob seemed to read her mind.

"Tori was in town for some meeting, so Laney and Andrea met up with her. It was a girl thing. I didn't want to go."

Molly finished cleaning the pot and turned it over on a paper towel to dry. There were no filters and not enough ground coffee in the tin for more than a cup. Thankfully, Travis was successful in his quest.

Ten cups of coffee later, Molly was still awake. She had leafed through every magazine in the room. "What time is it?" she asked of no one in particular.

"A little after five," said Rob, without looking at his watch. "I wish someone would tell us what's going on."

When the door opened half an hour later, the doctor stepped into the small room. Molly stood up, set her jaw, and put her hands together, ready for the worst.

"She's stable. We were able to stop the bleeding. We had to remove her spleen."

"Then she's going to be okay?" asked Rob.

"We're not out of the woods yet." The doctor motioned the three to sit down. Molly and Travis moved to the loveseat. Rob and the doctor sat on the chairs facing them. "Mrs. Camden suffered damage to her right leg. She has several broken bones in her right arm and rib cage as well. We've called in Dr. Toma, the premier orthopedic surgeon around here. We won't know the full extent of her injuries for a few days. There's possible damage to the spinal cord. We will just have to take it one day at a time."

"Can we see her?" Molly asked.

"She is in recovery right now. We'll move her to intensive care shortly. I can let you see her through the glass for a few minutes once she's there, but you can't go in yet."

Peering through the glass, Molly could barely stand the ache in her chest. She drew her hand over her heart, watching as her daughter lay on the ICU bed. Laney's face was swollen. A large tube was in her mouth. Smaller tubes ran in and out her left arm and hand. Wires connected the young woman to an array of machines lining the wall behind the bed.

Rob stood at the glass partition, his hand touching the glass in a futile attempt to touch his wife. His mouth pulled tight as he fought back tears.

Molly looked to her own husband. Tears were flowing freely down his cheeks.

"She is breathing on her own," the nurse on duty said. "That's a good sign."

Slowly, the tubes will come out, and she'll open her eyes. It's a process. Molly tried to comfort herself.

"Make yourselves comfortable," the nurse suggested as she led the three to a new, larger waiting area down the corridor from the ICU. "If you need anything, just touch the help desk button on the phone. To make an outside call, dial seven first."

So much information, when all Molly wanted to hear was that Laney would be okay. She bit her cheek to keep from crying as she took in their new surroundings. This room was fitted with at least ten of the comfortable brown chairs. Mounted in the corner of the room was a television. A remote rested on a table. Would there be news of the accident on the local morning news? Would she have the strength to watch it if it were?

A uniformed deputy sheriff came through the door before anyone had a chance to sit. He introduced himself as Hank Steadman and shook hands with Travis and Rob. "How's your wife, Mr. Camden?"

"She's in the surgical ICU. They stopped the internal bleeding, but the doctor said she's not out of the woods yet."

"They're a good bunch of doctors here," he assured them.

"Officer, was it ice on the road?" Travis asked.

"I'm still investigating." Deputy Steadman turned to Rob. "It was the middle of the night, Mr. Camden. Did you know where your wife *was* at that hour?"

Molly's head jerked up. What was this man insinuating? Trouble between Rob and Laney?

"She went out with some friends for dinner and then called me from River Rats to say she was on her way home," Rob stated without reservation.

Deputy Steadman made a notation in his book. "I should have my initial findings filed today, but you probably won't be able to pick up a copy of the typed report until Monday at the station."

Travis stepped closer to the officer. "But it was the ice, right?"

"We should be able to finish the full investigation next week." The man continued to address Rob. "The final report will be filed once we have all the details. You can pick up personal items at the station."

The officer shifted. "Look, I hate to ask, but did you know the other woman in the car with Mrs. Camden?"

"The other woman?" asked Rob.

Deputy Steadman looked at his notes. "A Victoria Johnson."

"Tori was in the car?" Molly asked. Laney wasn't alone. She hadn't dropped Tori off at some unknown destination before the accident.

"Yes, ma'am. We have an Illinois driver's license for her; but so far, we haven't been able to contact anyone at her residence."

"I'm pretty sure she lives alone," said Rob.

"Her parents live in the St. Louis area," offered Molly. Tori's parents were quiet, unassuming, and likable. It was largely because of the Johnsons that Molly and Travis had decided to let Laney move off campus and into the house with her friends their junior year.

"Nancy and Paul. Their names are Nancy and Paul Johnson."

"Thank you. That should help."

"How is Tori?" asked Travis.

Officer Steadman studied the three faces before him. "I'm afraid she didn't make it. She was pronounced dead at the scene."

Molly's stomach clenched as the room spun. The brown chairs took on odd shapes and moved in circles before her eyes. "I need to sit down," she whispered, even as Travis grasped her arm and lowered her into one of the chairs. She had blamed all of her daughter's pain and suffering on Tori.

What was it the nurse had said about Laney? *She's breathing on her own.* Laney lying in the bed connected to all of the machines and paraphernalia in the room didn't seem so bad. She was breathing on her own. A good sign.

But Tori?

Tori wasn't breathing at all.

Chapter 2

AT EIGHT O'CLOCK IN THE morning, Molly called her friend Marianne, who was in charge of the church prayer chain, but the call went right to voicemail.

"Marianne, it's Molly. I have a prayer request. Laney was in an accident last night. Please put this on the prayer chain right away. She had to have surgery. They removed her spleen, and she's in ICU right now. Please pray for healing." Molly swallowed hard, willing herself to not cry. "And pray for the Johnson family, too."

Molly's voice cracked. A lump formed in her throat, and tears clouded her vision. She swallowed again. "Pray for them. Their daughter, Victoria—Tori—died in the crash. She was a friend of Laney's."

Laney had grown up in that church. She was married in that church. Everyone knew her and loved her there. But Laney had stopped attending during her last two years of college—another bad habit Molly had long attributed to her association with Tori and Andrea. Molly trembled as she ended the call and looked to Travis and Rob, who were on their phones.

"Lissa's on her way," reported Travis as he put his cell phone away.

"She's not driving all the way from West Virginia, is she?" The prospect of her younger daughter behind the wheel of a car made her shiver.

"Flying. She'll catch a plane in Pittsburgh. It's only an hour away from Morgantown. She said she'll get a friend to drive her to the airport."

Rob walked across the room to join them. "Well, I just got off the phone with my sister. The kids are still in bed."

"That's good," Molly mumbled.

"Hunter has a basketball game at the Y at eleven. Tammy will go ahead and take them to the game. It's probably best to try to keep their life as normal as possible, right?"

Molly tried to think, but she was tired. "What is Tammy going to tell them?" Her nine-year-old grandson would accept a reasonable explanation, but five-year-old Ellie would demand to know why her parents weren't there.

"I told her to say Mommy and Daddy are busy, so she's babysitting." Rob ran his fingers through his hair. "But what am I going to tell them? And how?"

Whatever he decided to tell them, he should do it soon. Tammy was young and single. She loved her niece and nephew, but one slip-up and she could needlessly upset the children.

"What time did you say Hunter's game is?" Molly asked her son-in-law.

"Eleven."

"I'll be here, so if you want to meet them at the Y . . . " Molly began. Rob looked at her, his jaw set and lips drawn tight, making Molly fidget. "Or you could stay here, and we could go," Molly quickly added.

"Tammy should be okay." Rob relaxed a bit but rubbed the side of his face.

"Someone has to tell them their mother was hurt in an accident," Molly contended. "I don't think that should be put on Tammy. She's young, and, well, she's not a mother."

Rob seemed to consider her words. The three sat in silence for a few minutes.

"Why don't we do this?" Travis offered. "Rob stays here. I'll take Rob's car, go to the airport to pick up Lissa. Molly, you go get the kids. Bring them to our house. It's closer to the hospital anyway, and you can explain what happened."

Me? No, Travis, don't suggest I be the one.

"That could work," Rob said. "I need to be here. I *have* to be here when Laney wakes up; and if the kids are at your house, I can just come there later. You'll be better at explaining anyway."

As much as Molly hated leaving her daughter's side, it made sense for her to be the one to take care of the children. Laney would like that. Still, what would she say?

"Okay. I'll just be honest, but not give them too much detail. I'll tell them that their mother was in a car accident; but their daddy and the doctors are at the hospital taking care of her, and she'll be okay. How does that sound?"

"Don't say anything about Tori," Rob added.

Did he think she was a fool? She would never upset her grandchildren like that. They didn't need to know someone had died. Anyway, did they even know Tori? Molly hoped not.

"What are you going to tell Laney?" Molly asked him. "I mean, she'll be weak. I don't know how she'll take the news about Tori."

"I think I should steer her away from that subject," said Rob.

"But what if she asks?" Travis frowned.

"I don't know," Rob shrugged. "Tell her the truth, I guess."

"I disagree," Molly said. "I mean, couldn't you just say something like, 'I haven't seen her,' or something like that? Something that isn't quite the whole truth?"

Rob's shoulders drooped, and he put his head down. "I don't know."

Travis moved toward the young man and rested his hand on Rob's shoulder. "Don't worry. When the time comes, you'll find the right words."

A few minutes later, Molly stood at the glass watching her daughter. "It's a new day, Laney," she said. "The sun is coming up, and we have a plan. I'm going to take care of the kids and be back before you know it. Lissa is on her way right now; and soon, she'll be here, too. You don't need to worry, honey. We'll take care of everything. I'm praying for you, Laney. I love you so very much." The young woman lay still in the metal bed, her eyes closed. Molly touched the glass.

On her way out, Molly nodded to the on-duty nurse. "Thank you." She had just enough time to go home, shower, and get to the game.

But leaving was hard. As Molly wove her way back through the emergency room toward her car, she noticed families huddled together in quiet conversations, people holding each other, an older woman wiping away tears. Her thoughts turned once more to Tori's mother, Nancy. Molly shook herself. Hunter and Ellie needed a confident grandmother right now, not a crumbling one. They needed gentle assurance and a strong hug.

Getting into her car, Molly hastily whispered a prayer that she would find the right words for Hunter and Ellie. Their safe and happy world was about to change. Forever.

Chapter 3

THE WEEKEND PASSED SLOWLY UNDER the dark clouds of the February sky. Though Hunter and Ellie begged her to take them to the hospital, she couldn't. Their mother remained unconscious in the ICU.

Molly was grateful Lissa was around. She helped entertain the two energetic youngsters. Rob stayed around the clock at the hospital. Molly took shifts with Lissa, Travis, and Rob's sister, Tammy, to sit with him in Laney's room or in the waiting area.

She worried about the effect all this was having on the children. And Rob. If they didn't take food to him, he wouldn't eat.

By Monday, some of the tubes had been removed from Laney's mouth. The swelling on her face was starting to go down, and her color was returning to normal. The splint and bandage on her right arm had been replaced with an inflatable cast. Anyone going into Laney's room had to wear gloves and a mask to prevent the spreading of germs.

Molly tugged at the mask covering her face and willed Laney to wake up.

Though the children had taken the news fairly well, Molly and Travis kept them home from school on Monday. She told them how excited she and Grandpa were to have them stay overnight for a few days. She encouraged Rob to come to the house that evening.

"You could use the break, and the children need to see you. I know it would make them feel better," Molly told her son-in-law. "Travis or Lissa or I will stay with Laney for you."

Rob was noncommittal. "I'll see."

She smiled as Rob let himself in the house that evening. "Hey, everybody."

"Daddy! Daddy!" the children cried as they rushed into his waiting arms.

"Grams said Mommy was hurt in the car, but I think she's having a baby. Right, Daddy?" Ellie asked. "Hunter said that's why Mommy went to the hospital the last time."

Rob looked at Molly, eyes wide.

She could only shrug. This was the first she had heard of this conversation. Rob sat down at the table with the children and explained that Mommy was hurt and needed rest.

"Does Mommy have to stay in the hospital forever?" Ellie wanted to know.

"Did she break her arm?" Hunter asked.

"Mommy doesn't have to stay forever. She has a few broken bones, but the doctor is helping her. She's sleeping a lot right now, so she can get well. She needs you to help her, too."

"I'll help," Ellie said.

"How can we help?" Hunter inquired.

"You can help Mommy by doing your best in school. Then she won't have to worry about you, and she can concentrate on getting better."

Molly smiled at Rob. Maybe she underestimated him.

Tuesday morning, Rob called. "She's waking up! She opened her eyes. I about fell off the chair! She looked at me. She looked straight at me."

Rob called again when the children were home that afternoon from school. Molly put him on speakerphone, and Rob reported that Mommy was getting better. Hunter had been skeptical about how his going to school could actually help his mother; but after talking with his dad, he sat down to finish his homework at the kitchen table while Molly threw a frozen pizza in the oven.

While the children were at school, Molly and Travis spent the days sitting with Rob, hoping to witness their daughter's recovery. Longing to hear her voice. They missed her one awake moment on Tuesday; and on Wednesday, they arrived just after she had opened her eyes and smiled. The rest of the day she lay sleeping—wired, tubed, and connected as before.

Late Thursday morning, Molly and Travis sat with Rob in her room.

"Thirsty."

Molly jumped at the sound of her daughter's hoarse voice. She pressed the button to summon the nurse. Rob leapt to Laney's side.

The attending nurse swabbed Laney's mouth and told the family they were not to give her anything to drink until a specialist checked to make sure she was swallowing properly.

Molly used the swab the nurse had provided, repeatedly apologizing for not being able to give her a drink. A few minutes later, Laney spoke once more.

"What happened?" Her voice was weak and raspy.

"You were in an accident, sweetheart, but you're okay," Rob told her.

"What . . . accident?" Laney asked, glancing first at Rob and then at her parents. "The kids?"

"The kids are fine. They're staying at your mom and dad's house. Lissa, too," Rob explained.

"Everything's going to be okay, Laney." Molly stroked her cheek.

Laney closed her eyes, sleeping once more.

She experienced short bursts of alertness scattered throughout the day. Sometimes, she studied whoever was sitting by her side but said nothing.

Deputy Steadman had been by the hospital twice since the accident.

"He really cares," Molly told her husband as the deputy spoke with Rob on the other side of the waiting room. The nurses were busy in Laney's room changing her dressings.

"I hope that's what it is," said Travis, his lower lip twitching. "I have a feeling Hank Steadman isn't here just to see how Laney's faring. I think he's still investigating."

Once the officer had left, Rob confirmed Travis's suspicions.

"I've already told him everything I know. He made me promise to call him when Laney is strong enough to give him a statement," Rob shared. "Can you believe that guy?"

"Does he know she's awake?" Molly asked.

"I don't know, and I don't care," Rob answered. "Even though Laney's awake and talking, she doesn't even remember the accident. Steadman can wait." He turned and headed back down the corridor to Laney's room.

Women from Molly's Bible study group soon learned Hunter and Ellie were staying with them. Every few days, someone dropped by the house with a meal for the family. If Molly was home when they arrived, they'd come in, offer words of encouragement, and pray with Molly.

"We're so sorry."

"If there's anything we can do . . . " Then the voices would trail off with uncertainty.

Their words were always strained, always guarded. How many times had Molly delivered such meals? How many times had she fumbled for the right words to say?

Molly appreciated the meals they prepared, though. She smiled at the beautiful cranberry chicken and rice she warmed in the oven, remembering the seemingly endless pasta dishes she had received from the same group when her mother died. A little variety helped.

When Rob called on Friday morning to report Laney was being moved to the step-down unit, Molly was ecstatic. "This has to be a sign she is getting better," she told Travis as he headed to work for the first time all week.

After dropping the youngsters off at school, Molly and Lissa found Laney resting peacefully in a regular hospital bed. Rob snored softly on the converted chair-bed.

The two decided to slip down to the hospital cafeteria for a cup of coffee.

Molly sipped her coffee. "What a week, huh? I haven't even asked you how school is going."

"It's great. My biggest struggle is the advanced statistics class."

"I thought you already took statistics," Molly said.

"That was an undergraduate course. I have to take an advanced course now."

"All that is over my head," Molly admitted. Lissa told her about a research project she was working on with her graduate group at WVU. Molly listened with a pang of guilt, realizing this was the first conversation she'd had with her younger daughter since she arrived nearly a week earlier.

"Is all of this going to put you way behind?" Molly asked.

"I'll be fine," Lissa assured her. "But if Laney continues to show improvement, I may go back for the church youth group Sunday night. I help a man named Mark with the kids."

"She's improving every day."

"Yeah, last night when I came up, she asked me if I had met a guy yet. Same old Laney." Molly was about to ask her if Laney had reason to ask such a question when a groggy-looking Rob walked through the cafeteria doors. Lissa stayed behind to keep him company while Molly ventured back to Laney's room.

Laney was still connected to that infernal machine. How could anyone rest with that insistent noise and beeping? An intravenous bag hung on a metal hook above her bed.

But Molly found comfort in Lissa's words. *Same old Laney.*

When Melissa and Rob came in a few minutes later, Laney's eyes opened. Her voice was still raspy and soft. "Lissa, what are you doing here? Aren't you going to the science fair?"

"Just wanted to see how you're doing, Sis."

"I think I had an accident." Laney looked confused for a moment, then closed her eyes.

Molly sighed. Not quite the same old Laney after all.

As the day wore on, Laney experienced moments of clarity, sprinkled with short naps. By afternoon, she was able to string several thoughts together and carry on a meaningful conversation.

"Were Hunter and Ellie in the accident, too?" she asked.

"No, honey," Molly assured her.

"Then why can't I see them?"

"Laney, you're in the hospital. We can't go dragging the kids in here," Lissa answered. Had she lost patience with her older sister?

"Oh, well, that makes sense," Laney responded. Laney did not remember the accident, and no mention was made of Tori. At one point, Laney asked for her purse.

"Oh, uh, I've been kinda busy." Rob looked at Molly.

"Did you need something, sweetie?" Molly asked.

"No, just wondered." Laney closed her eyes and slipped into another short nap.

Molly and Lissa drove to the sitter to pick up Ellie. Back at Laney's house, Lissa located Teddy Grahams for Ellie's snack, while Molly gathered some clothes for the children and checked Hunter's basketball schedule on the refrigerator. Ellie wanted to play upstairs in her room while they waited for Hunter's bus. Molly eyed the microwave. Three o'clock. Hunter's bus wouldn't arrive until quarter to four. "Sure, sweetie. Go ahead."

"How long do you think Laney will be in the hospital?" Lissa asked, sitting at the kitchen table and munching on one of the three cookies Ellie left.

"The doctor hasn't said." Molly picked up one of the small, bear-shaped cookies. "He ran more tests yesterday. They had to remove her spleen, you know."

Tears welled up in Lissa's eyes.

"It's okay, Lissa. She can live without her spleen. She'll just have to be very careful about infections and flu, stuff like that."

"It's not that, Mom. It's just that I look around at this old house. I remember when Laney and Rob bought it. She was so excited. How will she be able to live here if she's . . . if she's . . . "

"What, Lissa? If she's what?"

"If she's paralyzed."

"She's not paralyzed! Whatever gave you that idea?"

"The doctor. He said there was possible damage to her spinal cord."

Molly's mind raced back to the morning of the accident. Those had been the doctor's exact words. "Possible damage to her spinal cord." Molly reached across the table and took her daughter's hand. "He hasn't said any more about that, honey. And remember when she complained her leg was hurting? I'm pretty sure she wouldn't feel the pain if she were paralyzed. You'll see. Laney will be just fine."

Still, that night as they got ready for bed, Molly asked Travis about it.

"That's been on my mind all week." He sat down on the edge of the bed. "I asked her doctor about it yesterday morning, but he just said what he always says. Too early to tell anything."

Molly was reeling. She couldn't sleep. Paralysis hadn't crossed her mind. She willed herself to not think about it. Her own mother's voice echoed from the past: "Don't borrow trouble, Molly Mae. Worrying about what might happen won't change it." Unfortunately, the more Molly told herself that she shouldn't worry, the more she did.

She lay in the dark, praying for the sunrise.

Chapter 4

"GOOD LUCK, HUNTER!" MOLLY CALLED after her grandson as he and Lissa headed for the car. She kissed Travis a quick goodbye. "I'll be there as soon as I get Ellie ready."

"Maybe we should be wishing you good luck."

Ellie had started the morning in a bad mood. She didn't want her usual helping of cereal but requested—or demanded—waffles instead.

"We always have waffles on Saturdays," she whined.

Rather than argue, Molly dug her waffle iron out from beneath the seldom-used electric wok. The first batch was flat, but the second batch seemed light and fluffy.

"Yucky!" Ellie declared. "I like my mommy's waffles."

"You didn't even try them, Ellie."

"Yucky!"

"You have to eat something, honey, and we have to get going. We want to see Hunter play his basketball game, right?"

"No!"

Finally, she settled for a banana. At least it was a healthy choice. And it was better than fighting with a kindergartner.

Ellie threw a tantrum over putting on her socks and shoes. She cried when Molly brushed her hair. Molly finally wrestled the mass of dark hair into a ponytail holder, tangles and all.

By the time they arrived at the YMCA parking lot, both were tired and frustrated. They walked into the gymnasium minutes before the game was to start. Suddenly, Ellie pulled away from her and raced across the shiny wood floor. Ellie flew into her dad's arms.

"Rob, I didn't expect to see you here."

"I know, but Laney woke up around five and cried when she realized it was Saturday and she was missing Hunter's game. I promised I would come video it for her. My sister's with her now."

A loud air horn sounded as Molly sat beside Travis. Lissa took a picture of Hunter as he lined up on his side of the court. Ellie sat on the floor happily coloring with another little girl and totally ignored Hunter's endeavors in the game.

Travis shouted, "Nice assist! Way to go, Hunter."

Molly looked around. The event was like a soothing balm to the family's raw emotions. There was inexplicable rest in not being solely responsible for the children. For the first time in seven days, Molly was able to relax.

"Go, Hunter!" she cheered. "Look, Ellie; your brother made a basket!"

Ellie looked up at her grandmother. "I want to go home."

Ellie's mood had to be because her life was so unsettled. *I'm having a tough time, and I'm an adult.*

Rob was busy videoing the game. Hunter faced the camera and said, "Did you get that, Dad? Did you see my basket?"

Rob gave him a thumbs up.

Last night's nightmares of Laney being paralyzed were surely unfounded. Rob wouldn't be here laughing and playing with his children if he was worried about Laney's condition. Accidents happen. The worst was behind them.

After the game, Rob hugged Hunter and congratulated him on the basket. He swooped Ellie up on his shoulders and led the way out to the parking lot. Molly, Travis, and Lissa were close behind, enjoying the chatter of the children as they both tried to talk at once to their dad.

Rob set Ellie down near the car and turned to Molly. "I'm going to run by the sheriff's office and pick up Laney's things." Hunter heard Rob, looked down, and kicked a piece of gravel loose on the pavement.

"Hey, why don't the rest of us take Hunter out to celebrate his win?" Travis suggested as he mussed Hunter's hair.

Hunter grinned. "Can we?"

"Since I'm going to fly back to Pittsburgh tomorrow after church," Lissa began, "I think I'll bow out of lunch. I want to sit with Laney a bit. That is, if I can take your car, Mom."

Molly buckled Ellie in the back seat of Travis' car and prepared herself for Pizza Palace with a hefty dose of video games.

"I want to go to Skyline Chili," Hunter announced.

Hunter's choice, famous for its Cincinnati-style chili served on spaghetti, surprised her.

"I don't want chili," Ellie stomped. "Why does Hunter always get to choose?"

It took them twenty minutes of persuading, prodding, and promising ice cream to get her to agree to Skyline. Once there, Ellie ordered spaghetti with no sauce, which she ate heartily and declared to be her favorite.

As the foursome loaded into the car to go for ice cream, Travis received a text message. He sent a quick reply. Molly studied him as he set the phone between them.

"Rob" was all he said, offering Molly a weak smile and revealing nothing. "Hey, kids, let's just get ice cream at the drive-thru so we can get home and watch a DVD."

"Can we watch *Little Mermaid?*" Ellie asked.

"No way. I want to watch *Transformers.*"

Travis was quiet during the short ride home. The movie argument between Hunter and Ellie kept Molly occupied, though she wondered what Travis had on his mind.

Her own car was parked in the drive. "I thought Lissa would still be at the hospital with Laney." Travis didn't respond.

Lissa greeted them at the door with a smile for her niece and nephew. "Hey, you guys!" She turned to Travis and Molly. "I'll keep them busy, Dad."

"I told them they could watch a DVD."

"What's going on?" Molly asked as Travis guided her back to the car.

"I'm not sure. There was something in the deputy's report Rob wants to discuss with us. We're supposed to meet him at their house."

"But what is it?" Molly asked.

"I have no idea. He just said come and leave the kids with Liss."

"It sounds bad, don't you think?"

"I have no idea, Molly. We'll find out when we get there."

"What if that Officer Steadman gives her a ticket or something? I mean since the accident was bad . . . Do you think—?"

"Molly," Travis interrupted. "I said I have no idea what this is about. Stop with the guessing and worrying. Please!"

Molly gritted her teeth and pulled her mouth tight. She was not a child to be reprimanded.

A few minutes later, in total silence, Travis and Molly walked in to find Rob sitting on the living room sofa, staring out into space. His face was stained with tears. Looking up at his in-laws, Rob lifted his copy of the report to Travis. His hand shook. Travis scanned the form. Molly tried to look over his shoulder.

"Ice and snow on the roads. Just as I suspected."

"There's more," Rob said.

"Blood alcohol levels of the driver likely contributed to the accident," Travis read. "What?" Travis and Molly cried out in unison.

The words hung heavy in the air. Molly couldn't breathe.

"The deputy I talked to said they haven't cited her with a DUI yet; but if they do, she could face charges of vehicular homicide."

Molly sat, and Travis joined her. Vehicular homicide. A cold silence engulfed all three.

Rob exhaled slowly. "I don't know what to do."

Travis scratched his head. "Maybe I missed something." He scanned the report again. "I think we should get a lawyer to look at this, Rob."

"What about Charlie?" suggested Molly. "He goes to our church, and he's a good lawyer."

Rob nodded. "I remember him from our wedding."

Charlie Brown. Definitely an unfortunate name for a lawyer Molly had thought when she first met the man. But Charles Emerson

Brown, III, took pride in his name. It was, as he often quipped, at least memorable.

Travis called Charlie's house and left a message on the answering machine. He then suggested they draft a list of questions to ask the lawyer. Rob calmed as the men discussed their plan.

Molly picked up the report. The date and time of the accident were recorded along with the 911 call from a local man who came upon the scene moments after it happened. Deputy Steadman's accident report was filled with details about the location of the car, measurements taken from the road, and a description of a cement culvert located at the turn.

The car had flipped and rolled. Molly shuddered. She wasn't sure she could read this. Yet her eyes were drawn to the paper in her hands.

Rescuers used the jaws of life to remove Laney from the mangled mess. Her legs were pinned by the car's framework and dashboard. Molly cringed at the thought of her daughter trapped in the mass of twisted metal.

Tori had been thrown partway through the windshield before the car rolled on top of her.

Molly stopped cold. She hadn't thought about Tori since the morning of the accident. Had the Johnsons been contacted? Surely if they had come to town, they would have come to the hospital or called to check on Laney.

But then, maybe they had seen the accident report. This report. The report Molly held in her hand. The report that suggested that her own precious Laney—not Tori at all—was to blame for Tori's death.

"I'm, um, going to go pick out some church clothes for the children. They'll need them for tomorrow and . . . " Once upstairs, Molly sat on the side of Ellie's bed.

"Why, God? Why is this happening?"

The pain she experienced this past week was one thing. But a new pain surged within her. The accident had seemed to be something that happened *to* Laney, but this? Laney had brought all of this suffering on herself.

And on them.

All of them. Rob, Hunter, and Ellie. Travis, Lissa. *Everyone* who loved her. They were all hurt by choices Laney made. Molly sagged beneath her disappointment. Laney had intentionally been vague about that evening. She had *planned* to go out and drink with her friends.

Laney had effectively put her parents in a little box, only to be taken out at her convenience. Only when she needed something. *Like someone to pick her kids up from school on a cold Friday in February so she could go to some bar on the river.* Molly shuddered beneath the weight of her own anger. Laney loved her parents—Molly was sure—but it had always hurt to be restricted to such a limited role in her life. Why couldn't they have a true friendship like she'd shared with her own mother? Where was that? Why didn't Laney want that kind of relationship?

She and Lissa were comfortable together. Was the reason they were closer because they both went to church? Lissa's values were centered on her relationship with God.

Laney was more interested in what other people thought of her. People like Tori and Andrea. Surely, Tori and Andrea had pressured Laney into drinking. Right?

No, resentment wouldn't help. And neither would making excuses. The problem was in Laney. Laney was thirty-two years old. She made her own decisions—the consequences of which would follow her for the rest of her life.

And what about Andrea? No one had heard anything from her all week. Why hadn't she checked on Laney?

Vehicular homicide. It sounded as if Laney had set out to murder her best friend. Is that what Andrea thought? That Laney had murdered Tori? Molly shivered. The thought was inconceivable.

Molly grabbed a corduroy jumper and turtleneck for Ellie and a pullover sweater and navy blue pants for Hunter. She threw the clothes, socks, and shoes in a canvas bag she found in Hunter's room and came down the steps in time to see her husband praying with Rob.

Molly didn't know how much stock Rob put in prayer, but she was happy to see him bowing his head with Travis. Rob had grown up in the church but, as an adult, had never seemed to have a need for God in his life.

Like Laney.

Molly sat down on the bottom step as the men prayed. She watched in silence for a while, then whispered her own silent prayer. "Please, God, please help us get through this. Don't let me say something to Laney I'll regret later. Lord, I feel so sick inside. And Rob. Poor Rob. God, please make this nightmare go away."

Chapter 5

MOLLY SUGGESTED THEY ATTEND THE second, more contemporary church service. They could have a leisurely breakfast, go to the eleven o'clock service, and slip out early before too many people crowded in on the family with unanswerable questions. They would stop by the hospital, pick up sandwiches, and still have Lissa to the airport by one.

Tammy agreed to take care of the kids so Travis and Molly could meet Rob at Charlie Brown's home office at two. It would be tight.

Rob called at eight o'clock Sunday morning. The doctor had just left the room. He had given permission for the children to visit their mother, one at a time, for five minutes each.

Molly hurried the children through a breakfast of cereal and fruit. Lissa took charge of getting Ellie ready, while Travis challenged Hunter to see which of the "men" in the house could get ready first. Lissa was still brushing Ellie's hair in the car as they made their way to the hospital.

"Yes, you get to see your mommy today, but for only a few minutes. When it's time to leave, you have to leave right away, okay? Don't argue or cry because that would make her feel bad, okay?" Molly tried to think what else she should say. *How do you prepare children for a five-minute visit when they haven't seen their mother for a whole week?*

"You can go first, Ellie," Hunter said. Both children stood in the prep area. Even though the adults were no longer required to scrub and wear a mask, the doctor required the children do so. They had both been at school all week. Without a spleen, and with her body still healing, Laney was at risk. An IV still delivered a concoction of preventative drugs, but the doctor didn't want to take any chances.

The door to the prep area opened. Ellie hid behind her grandmother.

A petite young brunette greeted them with a smile. "I'm Ms. Smith. I'm the Family Services Coordinator." She looked at Hunter and Ellie. "I bet you have a lot of questions about what's happening with your mom." She told them about their mother's bruises and bandages. She showed them a photo of the equipment in the hospital room and told them about each piece.

Molly silently thanked God for Ms. Smith's understanding of children. She had just the right words.

The young woman bent down to help Ellie shape the nose clip of the paper mask to fit her small face. "If you have more questions, just ask me." Ms. Smith stood and carefully adjusted Hunter's mask. "There you go. Wow, you look like a young doctor."

Hunter's eyes grew wide.

"And when you finish your visit, you each get a special gift your mom picked out for you."

"Will my picture make Mommy sick?" Ellie held out a crayon drawing.

Ms. Smith studied the picture. "This is beautiful," she said appreciatively. "I think this picture will make your mommy feel better. You better give it to her. I'll get some tape to put it up on her wall."

Ellie visited Laney for exactly five minutes and returned with Ms. Smith without complaint. "Look what I got." She held a book of paper dolls. Hunter returned five minutes later with a word puzzle book.

Lissa and Molly stepped into Laney's room before leaving for church. Laney was smiling and alert. "Seeing my kiddos was the best medicine ever."

"Mommy said for us to be good at church," Hunter was telling Travis when Molly returned to the waiting area. She had expected tears and a struggle to leave the hospital.

"Whatever they are paying Ms. Smith, it isn't enough," Molly whispered as they loaded the kids into the car.

Molly slipped into the back of the church after dropping off the kids at their classes. Travis started toward the front where they usually sat, but she tugged at his arm. "Back here," she whispered as she moved toward the corner. She didn't look forward to meeting with her church friends this morning. A few people she knew had already glanced their way. Was she imagining it, or did everyone know by now that Laney had been drinking?

One of the church leaders began making announcements. Molly let her mind wander. She was fifty-nine years old and couldn't remember a time in her life when she hadn't been in church. She stared at the backs of the heads of friends she had known over the years. She could name most of the people in the room. They were her "church family." Yet today, Molly felt out of place.

Travis nudged his wife. Molly looked around to see everyone standing as the congregation began to sing. She mouthed the words without a sound. Travis' booming voice sounded natural—comfortable and at home. But it felt like betrayal. In this storm of their life, Travis was at peace with God. Why didn't he feel the same discomfort she was experiencing? How could he stand there and sing about God's power and protection? Where was God a week ago when Laney was driving on Old Creek Road?

Molly looked down at the paper she held in her hand. Communion would be served to believers after this song. What was it the Bible said about receiving communion? Something about a worthy manner? Molly had memorized the verse as a child. She had memorized the entire list of fifty verses that year to win a prize.

Now, she couldn't remember a single one of them.

Well, it didn't matter. She was angry with God and was pretty sure that wasn't part of "a worthy manner."

"I need to go to the bathroom," she whispered to Travis. "I'll check on the kids while I'm out." Molly slid past Travis and Lissa.

"You okay, Mom?" Lissa whispered.

"Yeah, fine," Molly lied. "Just going to the bathroom, then to check on the kids."

Molly made her way to the area Pastor Haynes called the atrium. In the first building located on this site, the area outside the sanctuary had been smaller and called the vestibule. That was okay. The pastor also called the sanctuary an auditorium. Everything seemed to change.

Two ushers stood near the exit door, engaged in conversation. One spotted Molly and headed down the corridor toward her. Molly pretended not to see him and moved quickly to the ladies' room. So that she could honestly say she had, she made a point of using the facilities. Standing in front of the cold, white, porcelain sink, she glared at herself in the mirror. Finally, she washed her hands and struggled to pull out a brown paper towel stuck in the metal dispenser.

Molly slumped down on the small bench near the door. She was alone. So alone. Had she ever felt more alone in her life? How could this be happening? "I've had enough, Lord," Molly said out loud. She leaned her head against the wall and closed her eyes.

Molly waited, but no revelation from God came. No comfort. No peace.

Seeing no one as she peeked out the door, she slipped down the back stairs and looked in on the classrooms her grandchildren occupied. Each was engaged in a Bible story being delivered by a volunteer teacher.

Communion time must surely be over. Molly made her way back to the sanctuary. Or auditorium. Let them call it whatever they liked. What did it matter now? Molly hoped the sermon would be something from the New Testament. She needed a message of hope and joy today of all days. Pastor Haynes was already speaking when she returned to her seat.

"Kids okay?" Travis whispered.

"Doing great."

Travis handed her his open Bible. He pointed to the text in First Kings. *Humph! Old Testament. What could possibly be here for me?*

"Look at what it says in verse four," Pastor Haynes said. "This is Elijah talking to God. 'I've had enough, Lord.' Elijah is saying what we've all said at one time or another. But let's look at verse five."

Molly pulled the text close to her. First Kings, chapter nineteen. She couldn't believe what she was hearing. Hadn't those been her words just moments ago? Was God listening?

"God sends an angel to Elijah," Pastor Haynes said. Molly looked at the insert in her bulletin. In the sermon outline, the pastor had written three R's under the gifts the angel offered to Elijah. The heading read, "Gifts of Grace from God."

"Elijah feels separated from God. What does God give to Elijah through this angel? First, He gives him rest. Then He gives Elijah refreshment. Finally, He offers a retreat," Pastor Haynes continued.

She so needed these. Travis, too. Molly looked over at her husband. He had been balancing work, visits to the hospital, and helping with the children. Stomach twisting, Molly admitted this was the first time she'd thought of her husband's needs in a week. Her focus had been solely on Laney.

"Look closely," Pastor Haynes said. He was already on to verses eleven and twelve. "God has control over everything. He sends a powerful wind, an earthquake, and even a fire. But look again. God speaks to Elijah in a gentle whisper. I wonder how many times we're waiting for God to get our attention with a bolt of lightning. Sometimes, God whispers."

When Pastor Haynes began his final prayer, Molly closed her eyes and offered her own. As she confessed her earlier doubts, Molly realized she hadn't truly prayed since the accident. Yes, she'd breathed a request here and there. *Please help Laney.*

Please be with the doctors.

Please make all of this go away.

A simple sentence offered on the run. Begging, really.

Travis' hand on her shoulder drew her attention. The rest of the congregation was standing to sing. Molly continued to sit, her face in her hands. Travis held his hand steady. She loved this man. She craved his strength.

After the service, Lissa retrieved the children from their classes while Molly and Travis answered the inevitable questions, received numerous hugs, and promised to call on their friends if they needed anything. Molly enjoyed the love and support her church family offered. She marveled at how her attitude had changed over the course of one hour.

No one mentioned Laney driving under the influence. No one spoke of Tori. Most of the questions were about Laney's recovery or Rob and the children. Maybe Laney's drinking wasn't public knowledge after all. Maybe God *would* make all of this go away. The thought of meeting with Charlie later in the afternoon brought with it a sense of renewed hope.

Any peace Molly had experienced faded as she stood on the sidewalk of the airport's departure drop-off. Travis pulled Lissa's bags from the trunk of the car as she hugged Hunter and Ellie goodbye.

"I'm going to miss you so much." Molly bit her lip.

"It's okay, Mom. I'll be back before you know it."

Lissa was a good listener and offered a perspective that helped Molly stay grounded. Molly knew Hunter and Ellie would miss Aunt Liss as well.

"I'll call every day and return soon."

"Don't rush back," Travis advised. "Wait until Laney gets home. I don't like the idea of you driving here by yourself in this February weather."

"Didn't you see the groundhog report, Dad? We're in for an early spring. But I promise if it's bad weather, I'll rethink that whole idea or get someone to come with me, okay?"

On the drive back, Molly and Travis were silent. Hunter and Ellie chattered in the backseat and played with the books they received at the hospital. The meeting with Charlie crowded Molly's mind.

She wanted to hear him say this was all a big mistake.

Chapter 6

THE MEETING AT CHARLIE BROWN'S home office didn't offer Molly the assurance she hoped for. He asked more questions than he provided solutions. He carefully explained Ohio's drunk driving laws. The likelihood of a charge against Laney seemed inevitable.

The term "drunk driving" made Molly cringe. "Driving under the influence" somehow seemed less insulting.

Charlie kept Rob's copy of the accident report and promised to call him after he did a little investigating on his own. "For one thing," he noted, "the actual blood alcohol level isn't recorded in this initial report. I'll run by the sheriff's office tomorrow and see what I can find out." Charlie led them in prayer before they left.

"Lord, we're trusting You in this. We just need to ask You now for wisdom and guidance," Charlie prayed. "Please help me, Lord. Help me to help Laney. And Rob. You only want what's best for us, Lord. Show us the way."

Molly looked up to see Rob, his head still bent and eyes squeezed shut. He looked up, thanked Charlie for his help, and shook his hand.

Once they were home, Molly fixed a fresh pot of coffee and poured a glass of iced tea for Rob. She pulled a tin of cookies from the pantry and set them in the center of the kitchen table. No one reached for them.

"Have you heard from Andrea at all?" Molly asked Rob.

"Not a word," Rob mused. "You would think she would have at least called."

Maybe. Maybe not. Not if she, too, blamed Laney. Molly rubbed her neck.

After spending a couple of hours with Hunter and Ellie, Rob left for the hospital. A light snow was beginning to fall. Travis built a fire in the fireplace. The children didn't have school the next day in celebration of President's Day, so Rob had agreed they could stay up an hour later than usual.

The kids talked Travis into setting up the electric train set he usually reserved for under the Christmas tree. They were in the midst of pulling the train cars and houses out of the boxes when Rob called. Laney was craving a chocolate milkshake. The nurse on duty said that would be acceptable for her liquid diet, but the hospital cafeteria wasn't open Sunday evenings.

Twenty minutes later, Molly walked into Laney's room with two chocolate milkshakes from a McDonald's drive-thru.

Andrea was standing at the foot of the bed. Only family was supposed to be allowed in the step down unit. How had she gotten past the nurse's station?

"I'm so sorry I couldn't get here sooner," she was saying. "I left early on Saturday for a meeting in Dallas with a client. Evan called me when he read about the accident in the paper."

"That's okay," Laney said sweetly. "I couldn't even have company at first."

"I just got back in town last night. I rerouted through St. Louis so I could go to Tori's funeral. It was really nice, and her mom and dad wanted to know how you were doing."

No! Molly gasped and held her breath.

Rob looked quickly at Laney. The damage was done.

Laney paled. "Tori's *funeral?*"

Andrea looked first to Rob and then to Molly, slow realization creeping over her face that Laney was unaware of Tori's death.

Until this moment. Molly studied her daughter. Now, Laney clearly understood that Tori had died in the same accident that had created this nightmarish week for her. She may not remember details, but she felt the intense pain of that horrible night at once.

Andrea stammered a moment, seeking the right words. Finding none, she turned and darted out of the room.

Tears flowed down Laney's face.

Rob moved closer to her, leaning in close and pulling her into his arms.

Molly just stood there a moment, the cardboard tray of milk-shakes in her hands. Then, as quickly as Andrea had left, Molly set the milkshakes down on the table beside Laney's bed and headed down the hall. She wanted with all of her heart to stay and comfort Laney, but she knew Rob would do that.

Right now, Andrea was hurting as well. Something in her told Molly she needed to offer comfort to her daughter's friend. She found Andrea leaning against the wall near the elevators sobbing.

"I thought she knew," she cried when she saw Molly. "I would never hurt her. I am so sorry."

Molly put her arms around the young woman.

"She doesn't remember anything about the accident. You didn't know. She had to find out sometime." Even as she spoke, Molly wasn't sure why she was there. Her daughter's pain must be unbearable right then.

Maybe God intended for her to be here, standing in this sterile, white hallway, holding a woman the same age as her daughter—the same woman she had made disparaging remarks about earlier that day. She felt no anger now, which surprised her. All she felt was heartbreak at the way the events of the previous weekend had changed the lives of so many people forever.

Molly guided Andrea to two empty chairs in an alcove just beyond the elevators.

"We met at an Italian restaurant for dinner; then Laney and Tori went to River Rats."

"You didn't go with them?" How little she knew of the events of that dreadful Friday evening.

"Oh, not me. Since I became a wife and mother, I guess I just don't find bar-hopping all that fun anymore." Andrea's eyes widened. "Uh, I mean, mostly because I had to get up in the morning for an early flight to Dallas."

"It's okay, Andrea. You don't need to protect Laney. She made her own choices."

"Tori can be . . . I mean, she could be awfully persuasive, you know. I keep thinking maybe things would have been different if I had gone with them."

"You can't think like that. Maybe things would have been worse. You don't know." Molly looked down the hall toward Laney's room.

"Someone from the sheriff's office called our house. He wants to ask me some questions. What should I tell him?" Andrea was clearly worried she might once again say the wrong thing and cause more hurt.

Molly's mind raced. Deputy Steadman was obviously completing his investigation. Andrea could tell him she thought it wasn't Laney's fault. She could tell him how wild Tori could be. Maybe with Tori's track record for getting drunk, Deputy Steadman would see that all of this was somehow Tori's doing. The accident report didn't mention that Tori had also been drinking. Was there a blood alcohol level recorded for her? Maybe she had been the one driving.

No, the accident report was clear that Laney had been cut out of the driver's seat. Maybe Tori grabbed the wheel and caused Laney to lose control. Andrea could tell the deputy how unpredictable Tori could be. She could suggest several possibilities.

In the end, she knew exactly what Andrea should say.

"Just tell him the truth," Molly advised. "Just tell him the truth. That's all you can do." The peace she'd experienced at church that morning returned. Only the truth honored God. "Andrea, before you go, would it be okay if I prayed with you?"

"I'd like that, Mrs. Tipton."

Molly held Andrea's hands in her own. She praised God for Andrea and her husband and children. She asked God to heal Laney's body and her heart. She prayed for Tori's family. She prayed from her heart.

When she finished, Andrea gave her a warm hug and left with a promise to call after she spoke with the sheriff's office.

"I don't know how, but I'll be here for Laney," Andrea said as she entered the elevator. "Tell her I'm sorry. Tell her I love her."

Molly smiled. Laney was loved. Andrea didn't blame her for Tori's death. As Molly turned toward Laney's room, her thoughts wandered back to that moment in the hallway when she and Andrea prayed.

Heal Laney's heart?

"Heal my own, Lord," she whispered into the shadows of the cold hospital corridor.

Chapter 7

BY THE TIME MOLLY RETURNED home from the hospital, the children were in bed. She fixed herself a cup of hot chocolate, joined Travis at the kitchen table, and explained all that had transpired. It was snowing heavily now. Hunter and Ellie would undoubtedly want to spend their holiday on the sledding hill.

"I tried to pray with her and Rob before I left, but she told me to leave her alone."

Travis nodded. "She needs time to process this."

Molly was surprised to awaken rested. She had climbed the stairs last night with the fragments of a plan forming in her mind; but once in bed, Molly slept through the night for the first time since the accident.

As expected, the children were anxious to take their sleds to the park. Travis headed to work, so Molly was the one to load the sleds, prepare a thermos of hot cocoa, bundle the children in their winter gear, and make the drive through the white blanket of snow covering their neighborhood to the sledding hill. How many times had she made this journey with Laney and Lissa in tow?

By the time the threesome reached the park, half a dozen cars were already in the lot. Hunter carried his sled; Ellie carried the

thermos of cocoa; and Molly pulled Ellie's sled up the small grade
from the parking lot to the top of the hill. Molly brushed the snow
off a bench situated near the top and helped Ellie with her mittens.
Hunter readied himself for his first run.

"I hope I don't have an accident like Mommy," Ellie said quietly.

Molly wanted to scoop her up and tell her to never take any
chances in life. But projecting her own fears onto her granddaughter wouldn't help either of them. Molly tried to keep her voice even.
"You'll be fine. Now go have fun!"

Hunter and Ellie laughed, squealed, and screamed their way
down the hill. Each hike up became slower and more labored as the
morning wore on.

After an hour and a half of play in the still-falling snow, the
children were ready to leave. Molly poured hot chocolate for each
of them, then loaded the sleds in the trunk of her small vehicle.
They'd been home just long enough to clean up and eat lunch when
Rob called.

Hunter and Ellie were excited to get to see their mother again.
But how was Laney? How was she faring today after learning about
the death of her friend? Molly couldn't ask Rob while the children
were within earshot. She had to trust that Rob's call was a sign that
Laney was emotionally stronger today.

"She's been sleeping most of the day," Rob told her as Hunter took
his turn visiting Laney. "I think it's her way of coping." He rubbed his
face. "We had a rough night—and an even rougher morning."

Before she could respond, Hunter returned, and Molly went back
with Ellie for her brief visit. Laney rallied for the five-minute visit,
then closed her eyes and fell back asleep.

"The doctor is making arrangements for a counselor to talk with her," Rob whispered as the children donned their coats in the waiting room.

On Tuesday, Molly had arranged a meeting with her manager to discuss her work schedule and tie up a few loose ends on her projects. Molly told Mr. Withers she could meet with him at eleven. That would give her enough time to take the children to school, pick up a few items at Laney's house, and stop by the hospital.

The snow caused the schools to be on a one-hour delay. The time would be tight, but Molly decided to follow through with the plan she had begun to form Sunday night. After dropping the children off at school, Molly headed straight to her daughter's house. She found several bottles of body lotion in Laney's bathroom cabinet, read the labels, and settled on something called Warm Vanilla Caramel. The framed picture of Hunter and Ellie playing in the woods at a local park had always been Laney's favorite. Molly took it from Rob's desk and set out to locate Laney's Bible. After a bit of searching, she found it under a magazine in a drawer by the bed.

Molly sat on the side of her daughter's bed and held the small Bible in her hands. She ran her fingers over the gold-embossed name on the cover: Alana Tipton. *We should have given her a Bible with her married name on it.*

She opened the book and read the inscription. "To Laney with much love, Mom and Dad." Her finger traced the date. Laney'd been ten years old.

Molly thumbed through the pages. Several passages were underlined. Molly smiled at a picture tucked inside the back cover—Laney and Lissa in their matching Easter dresses. Laney couldn't say "Melissa." She always referred to her baby sister as "Lissa." The name had stuck.

In the middle of the text, near the twenty-third Psalm, Molly found a folded piece of notebook paper. On the outside were printed the words "My Will." Molly unfolded the not-so-legal document. She remembered the day Laney wrote it. Molly's father had died from a heart attack. Travis explained to the girls how Grandpa had left each of them five thousand dollars in his will. He wanted them to use it for college. It was the first time Laney and Lissa had to deal with death up close.

"When I die, I want to be buried in the backyard next to Sam." Molly smiled as she read aloud the first line. Laney's pet hamster. After several amazing escapes, Molly had renamed him Houdini, but Laney loved Sam anyway.

"And I want Lissa to have all of my toys except my Pretty Pretty Pony because she has one. Mommy can have my Pretty Pretty Pony because she didn't have one of those when she was a little girl." Tears welled up in Molly's eyes. She carefully refolded the paper and tucked it back in Laney's Bible.

When Molly arrived at the hospital, Laney was alone in her room. She pulled the picture of the children out and handed it to her daughter.

"I brought you a few items from home." Molly set the Bible on Laney's table within reach.

Laney looked at the picture in her hand and set it next to the Bible. She was quiet, and her mood was dark.

"I brought you another little treat," Molly said brightly. She pulled the lotion from the bag and warmed some in her hands. Uncovering

Laney's feet, she began rubbing them gently. "Remember how you used to love to have a foot massage? I figured this would smell good and make you feel pretty." Molly chattered on. Laney turned her head away in complete silence. "Oh my, your feet are so dry, Laney. It's this arid hospital climate, you know."

Molly could sense the struggle in her own voice. Her plan should comfort Laney. Instead, it upset her more. The air was strained as Molly finished her task. Laney had a few marks on her legs from the accident. Her right leg was in a straight leg brace.

Molly lifted her gaze, about to speak again, but spotted tears in Laney's eyes.

"I'm sorry if I upset you. I . . . I love you, Laney. I just wanted to help."

Laney didn't respond.

Molly looked at her watch. 10:35. She looked to the door, willing someone—anyone—to walk in and somehow remedy the situation.

Finally, Molly leaned over and kissed Laney's cheek. "I've got to go now, sweetie, but I'll be back later."

Once in her car, Molly allowed herself to replay the visit in her mind. She was certain she had said nothing that should have hurt her daughter. *This is just a difficult time for her.*

That evening, Travis took Hunter to basketball practice.

"You boys go on," Molly told them as they headed out the door. "Ellie and I will stay behind and have dinner ready when you get home."

"I get to help?" Ellie danced around her grandmother.

"Yep, you can help me cook." Molly closed the front door. What could they come up with that didn't include macaroni and cheese?

Rob came home from the hospital in time to eat dinner with the children. He praised Ellie for her part in making the mashed potatoes. He helped Hunter with his homework and volunteered to supervise bath time. No mention was made about letting them visit Laney. Molly was anxious to talk with Rob about her state of mind; but as soon as the children were in bed, he headed back to the hospital.

She sat at the kitchen table. Her Bible rested on the counter by the telephone where she'd left it on Sunday. What had happened? She'd made all these promises to herself to get back into reading her Bible. Here it was Tuesday, and she hadn't given it another thought. Molly pulled out the sermon notes she had stuffed in the front pocket of her Bible cover.

Rest. Refreshment. Retreat. Molly longed for these; but even more, she wanted them for her family. She read the verses in First Kings again.

As she slid the sermon notes into her purse, she prayed for Laney's healing. Perhaps she would find an opportunity to share the sermon with her.

The snow was still on the ground Wednesday morning, but the roads were clear. Molly stopped by the hospital on her way to work.

Laney was awake. Her mood was still sullen, but she looked directly at her mother and spoke in an even tone.

"I was hoping you would come."

Molly smiled. Laney loved her. Needed her. Maybe she would just call into work and take the day off. Mr. Withers would understand.

Laney held out a small, white envelope with the hospital logo on it. "Could you mail this for me when you get to work? I don't know the address, but you can find it on the internet, I'm sure."

Molly looked at the envelope. *Mr. and Mrs. Paul Johnson.* "Would you like me to buy a nice card in the shop downstairs?" Perhaps she should buy two, since she had not sent one either.

"No, Mom, just mail it, okay?"

"Of course, sweetheart. I'll mail it right away." As Molly put the envelope in her purse, Laney fell silent. Again.

Travis had encouraged her to simply assure Laney of their love for her. He said to let Laney initiate any conversation.

Molly wasn't convinced. Surely, there were words she could leave her daughter to offer her comfort. From within the same pocket of her purse, Molly withdrew the folded bulletin from the church on which she had scribbled notes from the sermon.

"Laney, Sunday's sermon was wonderful. I brought the notes so I could share with you." Molly's enthusiasm was building. She reached for Laney's Bible. Quickly, she turned to the passage and read the verses she had found so comforting.

Laney turned her head away.

"I don't know, Laney; but when I read that, it just seemed to fit where we are right now." Molly searched for words. "We're like Elijah; we feel—well, sometimes God whispers. It's just that we have to listen. See?"

Molly held the Bible out for her daughter, thrilled when Laney reached for it.

Sudden anger clouded Laney's face. She shoved her old Bible back into Molly's hands, crumpling the pages.

"Yeah, well, Elijah could run away if he wanted to, couldn't he? He wasn't stuck here in this bed! Talk to *your* God about that!" Laney was shouting now.

Molly backed away, fighting the hot, threatening tears welling up within her.

Silence fell like an iron gate between mother and daughter. Laney again turned her head to the wall.

Tears flowed freely down Molly's cheeks. "I love you, Laney."

Laney's jaw was set.

Molly moved to the foot of the bed.

Laney was rigid. Her face, like a stone statue, was fixed into an expression of contempt.

Where did they go from here?

Chapter 8

SLUMPED IN THE SEAT OF her Honda, Molly cried until she felt empty and totally spent. God had seemed so close earlier that day. "Why God? Why is this happening?"

Molly couldn't go to work—she wouldn't be able to concentrate. She didn't want to go home, either.

Without making a conscious decision to do so, she drove away from the hospital toward Old Creek Road. The thought of seeing the site of the crash frightened her. Yet she had this inexplicable need to know. She kept driving toward the winding country road.

Snow still lingered on the ground, so Molly was grateful the roads were clear and dry. The sun shone brightly. She turned off of the main highway toward Landsboro. Old Creek Road was a mile beyond the village.

As she turned her car west onto Old Creek, Molly shuddered.

Even in the light of day, the road seemed narrow and dark. The pavement wound around the base of a series of hills on the left, with fast-flowing Black Creek on the right. Tall, barren trees, topped with a layer of snow, lined both sides of the road. Occasionally, a driveway leading to some hidden residence led off one direction or the other, marked only by a lone mailbox.

About two miles in, Black Creek banked off to the right, and the road made a sharp left up the hill, leaving the creek bed behind. The site of the accident was just beyond the hill. She slowed her car at the top, trying to picture the scene icy and covered with night's darkness. The road descended; and at the bottom, it veered sharply to the left.

The trees had been cleared here. From the crest of the hill, Molly could see the snow-covered rolling fields and pastures of the area farms. A sign showing the steep grade and sharp turn warned drivers of the danger ahead. Molly reduced her speed even more, barely creeping down the hill. Even though the sun was out and driving conditions were safe, she shivered at what lay ahead.

What was she doing there? The last thing Travis needed was for her to have a wreck.

Molly glanced quickly into the rearview mirror. No one. She longed to have this private moment, but this was a dangerous stretch of road. If something happened, how long would it be until someone found her?

Gripping the wheel and following the pavement, Molly scanned the terrain for a safe spot to pull over. A few yards from the road, a large post stood next to a metal gate crossing a long lane. *Probably a farm road leading to a hayfield or pasture.* Trusting it would not be in use today, she pulled in, parked the car, and walked the fifty feet or so back to the curve where Laney had lost control.

And Tori had lost her life.

Molly knew from the police report that locals called the small branch "Kline's Creek." It was a tributary to the much larger Black Creek. Faded blue and red plastic roses were wired to a wooden white cross and stuck into the ground near the creek in memory of an earlier victim of this deadly turn. Would someone put a cross here to remember Tori?

The concrete culvert looked harmless from this vantage point. Molly pulled her coat tightly around her.

She was no longer frightened. She didn't cry, yet a lump formed in her throat. A sharp pain shot through her neck and shoulders. She couldn't stop to analyze her emotions right now. She needed to leave.

Turning, she made her way back to her waiting car. She maneuvered the vehicle back onto the road toward home. For the past two weeks, she had been consumed with her daughter's well-being. She'd worried over the emotional toll Tori's death had taken on Laney.

Today, however, she came face-to-face with her biggest fear. Laney was separated from God. Her daughter may have lost control of the car thirteen days ago, but when had she lost control of her spiritual life?

The end of the week brought another snowstorm, resulting in two days of school closing for Hunter and Ellie. Travis took Thursday off as well and entertained Hunter by digging out Laney's old science fair project from the basement storage. Using the box of wires, light bulbs, and a battery, he taught Hunter how electrical circuits work. Ellie trailed behind Molly most of the day as she washed clothes and dusted furniture.

"I'm bored," Ellie whined.

"Do you want to play with your paper dolls?"

"No."

"Would you like to watch a DVD?"

"No." Ellie sighed.

"What *do* you want to do?" Ellie was frowning and sullen. Molly put the laundry basket down and sat on the basement step. She put her hand to the child's forehead. No fever. "Are you feeling sad, Ellie?"

"Uh-huh."

"Do you want to talk about how you feel?" Molly's mind raced. Could she remain calm and address Ellie's emotions without breaking down herself? Was Ellie missing her mother? Molly could handle that. She only hoped the little girl had not overheard adult conversations about accidents and lawsuits.

"Hunter said we aren't going to school tomorrow either."

"That's right. It was on the news. Is that why you're sad, sweetie?"

"Uh-huh. Tomorrow is One Hundreds Day. We were going to have a party."

"One Hundreds Day?" Molly had no clue what Ellie was talking about. "How about we have a party here?"

"It won't be the same. It won't be One Hundreds Day."

Molly took Ellie's hand as they climbed up the wood steps to the kitchen. "I think we should have a party anyway. And I think you and I should bake a batch of brownies for it. What do you think?"

Ellie brightened. "Can I stir?"

"Sure."

"And can Mommy come to the party?"

Molly scratched her head. "Not this time, kiddo; but as soon as she is able to eat them, we'll bake another batch and take a party to her. How does that sound?"

Snow fell continuously throughout the day. Molly was grateful Travis hadn't ventured into work. Rob called from the hospital.

"There's a winter advisory out. Level two snow emergency. Technically, I shouldn't have been on the roads, but there was no way I was going to stay alone at the house and leave Laney wondering."

Molly's heart melted. Rob was a good husband. She doubted her daughter truly realized how lucky she was to have him.

Lucky. Hmm. That wasn't a word Molly had thought of lately. While she had him on the phone, Molly asked Rob if he knew anything about a One Hundreds Day party.

"No, but maybe Hunter knows."

Of course. Why hadn't she thought to ask Hunter?

Friday, Molly stayed at home with the children, letting Travis and Rob brave the ice and snow. She wished Travis hadn't had to go into work, but at least the hospital was on his way.

He took his cell phone back into Laney's room so Molly could talk with her daughter.

"I love you, Laney." Silence.

Molly imagined her voice echoing awkwardly into Laney's room. "The children are building a snow family outside. Do you want me to get them so you can talk to them?"

Silence. "I tell you what, I'll take a picture of their snow people for you." Molly hoped she sounded upbeat.

Still, there was no response. A few minutes later, Travis came back on the line.

"I've never seen her this down before. I don't know what to do."

Molly could picture her husband pacing the floor of the hospital hallway.

"Maybe I should call Pastor Haynes," Molly said.

Surely, Pastor Haynes would have the right words to bring Laney back to her senses—return her heart to the Lord. Maybe through all of this, Laney would come back to church.

When she called the church, Kate, the church secretary, assured her that Pastor Haynes would put Laney at the top of his hospital visit list.

Travis would be safe at work soon. The children were busy working on their snow family—a mommy, daddy, and two children. There was nothing more she could do.

Finally, Molly ventured out to the porch to view the snow creations. She provided scarves, hats, and old gloves to dress the snow people. Much to the delight of her grandchildren, she took several pictures.

Hunter proved to be a wealth of information regarding One Hundreds Day. The day was a celebration of the one hundredth day of school.

"The little kids just do stuff like blow up one hundred balloons or something," he explained. "One time, one of my teachers had us write stories about being a hundred years old."

"What did you write?" Molly asked.

"I said that when I am a hundred, I will be a hero."

Molly pulled her grandson close to her side. "I think you're already a hero," she said.

"How?"

"Well, you look out for your little sister, and you help me and your grandpa. You do what you are supposed to do, like your homework. Heroes are people who do what's right."

Hunter beamed. Even though his life was a bit upside down right now, his expression gave her a glimpse of the insecure little boy inside who so needed assurance.

"I have an idea," Molly said to her grandchildren. "Let's make a list of one hundred things we are happy about. We can type it on the computer and print out a copy for Ellie to take with her to school when they finally celebrate One Hundreds Day. And we can keep a list to share with your mom and dad."

Charlie Brown called after lunch while the children were on only number sixteen.

"I tried to call Rob's cell, but got no answer. We need to talk. Is he staying at your house?"

"Pretty much. He told me he will be here by 5:30 tonight."

"Would eight o'clock be too late?"

"I'm sure that will work. I'll tell him you're coming."

The rest of the afternoon passed slowly. The impending meeting with the lawyer pushed aside Molly's short-lived good humor. She tried not to guess what he had to say. She told herself to be positive. Finally, as the children settled in to watch a DVD, Molly closeted herself in her bedroom to try to pray. "Lord, please let me feel comfort and peace again."

Molly opened her Bible, uncertain where to turn. She had started one of those read-through-the Bible-in-a-year programs in January but was already a few chapters behind when Laney's accident occurred. Now, Molly had all but abandoned her Bible reading. She felt like the Israelites who wandered about the desert must have felt:

knowing there is a God and a promise, but not quite sure how to reach either.

She turned to the concordance. *Peace. I know there is a verse about peace.* A long list of verses greeted her. The first phrase to catch her eye was " . . . seek peace and pursue it."

"Psalm 34:14," she said to herself, opening to the full text. *Turn from evil and do good; seek peace and pursue it.* Molly let her eyes travel up the page to the beginning of the chapter.

There was a notation under the chapter heading. *Of David. When he pretended to be insane before Abimelech, who drove him away, and he left.* Molly didn't know exactly the story to which the notation referred, but the sentiment made her think of Laney. Were Laney's sudden anger and cold silence merely a pretense to keep those closest to her at bay? Was it her way of coping with the realization that she was responsible for Tori's death?

Laney seemed determined to push God away.

Chapter 9

ROB PICKED UP THE CHILDREN earlier than expected. "My sister's making dinner for us tonight."

"I can fix dinner for all of us. You can even invite Tammy."

Rob turned his back to the family room where his children sat happily engaged in their DVD. He lowered his voice. "I don't want them to be here when Charlie comes. I asked Tammy to stay with the kids. I'll be back by eight."

The house was suddenly quiet. Molly picked up the toys and books scattered in the family room. She looked at the clock. Travis would be home in a little over an hour.

"Do good. Seek peace." Molly set the dining room table. Grandma Blevins advised her as a newlywed to always set the table first. She could still hear her grandmother's voice. "When your husband comes in from a hard day's work, he'll see the table and think dinner's almost ready."

Molly put two frozen chicken breasts to thaw in a bowl of hot water. She raced upstairs for a quick shower, changed into a pair of black slacks and a soft red sweater, and ran a brush through her hair. Returning to the kitchen, Molly pulled a box of rice and a can of crushed pineapple from the pantry. She cut the nearly thawed chicken into small chunks of meat and sautéed some chopped onion and garlic in olive oil. The water for the rice began to boil.

Chicken fried rice was one of Travis's favorite dishes, and one Hunter and Ellie considered "yucky." She had just cracked two eggs into the pan when Travis came walking through the door.

"Something smells great!" he said. "And the dining room table? What's the occasion?"

"I wanted to make you a special meal. Rob took the kids to their house, so it's just you and me. At least for a while."

Travis put his arms around Molly's waist and drew her close. "Do you know how much I love you?"

The dinner satisfied more than a physical hunger. Even with a CD playing softly in the background, the dining room seemed quiet. Restful. Questions about Charlie's upcoming visit loomed large, but the two managed to keep their conversation centered on the best parts of the day.

"Two of my project designs were approved and accepted by the city commissioners today," Travis said. "How was your day?"

"I'll show you!" Molly shared the pictures of the children with their snow family. "They had so much fun in the snow, Travis. And, oh! I finally found out what One Hundreds Day is all about." She told him about the list they were compiling.

After the table was cleared, the couple stood side-by-side at the sink in the kitchen washing the antique china plates by hand.

"Thank you for this," Travis said. "If I were making a list, having a nice, quiet meal with my wife is something I'd put near the top of it." A sense of peace washed over Molly. *Do good. Seek peace.*

Charlie arrived ten minutes before the hour. Rob was ten minutes late.

"I had to read three books to Ellie before I left," he apologized.

"Only three?" Travis asked. "You got off easy."

Molly served coffee as the men chatted about the Bearcats basketball season. When she joined them at the kitchen table, Charlie pulled a pad of paper from his briefcase then retrieved a pen from the depths of the leather case and looked at his audience.

"First, I need to tell you the sheriff's department has decided not to pursue a DUI charge." Rob, Travis, and Molly released a collective sigh of relief.

"So, she wasn't . . . " Travis bit his lower lip. " . . . drunk?"

"The numbers were borderline at best. They can't determine how much can actually be attributed to the alcohol and how much was caused by the weather and road conditions. That particular stretch of road has been the sight of several accidents over the years. Residents complain it's dangerous even without ice on the road."

"So, she won't be charged at all? It's over?" Molly shifted.

"I'm afraid it's not that simple. The sheriff's office is not going to charge her with a DUI, but they could still decide to charge her with failure to control the vehicle. That's unlikely, though, at this point. Like I said, it's a bad stretch of road. However, I need to warn you, the Johnsons could file a civil suit. No matter how you look at it, Laney was driving; there was an accident; and their daughter was killed."

"What do we do now?" Rob wanted to know.

"Absolutely nothing. We just have to wait it out. Whatever you do, don't let Laney admit any guilt. And by no means initiate any contact with the Johnsons."

Rob and Travis nodded in agreement, but Molly felt sick. She cast her eyes down, tracing the dark lines in the wood grain of the tabletop.

"I may have done something I shouldn't have done." Molly told them about the letter Laney asked her to mail to the Johnsons. "I thought it was a letter of condolence. I just did as she asked."

The men were silent. Her mind raced, remembering Laney's state of mind that day. *What was in that letter?*

"What's done is done," Charlie said. "We'll wait and see."

"If they sue, won't the insurance cover it?" Travis asked.

"We can hope they would settle for what the insurance offers, but I need to prepare you for the worst." Charlie looked at Rob. "They could potentially sue you for everything you own."

Rob's mouth fell open. "Everything?"

"I just need you to know the risks. How much liability insurance do you carry?"

"A million dollars. We just bumped it up last year. Our insurance agent said it was well worth the extra ten bucks a year."

"That's good," Charlie agreed. "The Johnsons are likely to file a claim. A million dollars? They may settle for that."

Rob pushed his fingers through his hair. He blinked hard and looked away.

"It'll be okay," Molly said. "We're here for you." She put her hand on Rob's shoulder.

"Besides that," Travis interjected, "they may never bring a suit."

"It's not that." Rob was openly crying now. "I just don't know how much I can take."

Rob stood up and paced around the kitchen, rubbing his forehead. No one spoke. Rob had been so strong, so supportive. Surely, he wasn't thinking about turning his back on Laney now? And for what? Money? She wished Travis would do something.

"You don't understand. Laney made me promise not to tell anyone yet, but I can't keep that promise." Rob looked to Travis, then to Molly. "The doctor ran tests." Rob paused.

Molly clenched her jaw and looked at her son-in-law.

"Laney is paralyzed." A single tear made its way down his cheek. Rob wiped his face with the back of his hand.

Molly felt as if she had been punched in the stomach. *Laney!* Travis paled. He looked at Molly, his eyes rimmed with tears. He cleared his throat and stared up at the light.

All Rob had been feeling over the course of the past weeks came out, his voice quavering. "Should I leave? Can I?" Molly buried her face in her hands.

The three sat and listened. Spent, Rob sagged into one of the vacant chairs. Molly reached across the table and put her hand on his. Only Charlie found his voice. He began to pray.

Molly could hear Charlie praying, but the words escaped her. He called on God to help them, but all Molly could think was God had put them in this mess to begin with. The voice in her head was screaming. *Why? Why Laney? Why paralyzed, God? Hasn't she suffered enough? Why are You doing this to us? Why?*

Eventually, Charlie and Rob headed out, leaving Molly and Travis to face a sleepless night. Long after the coffee cups had been cleared, the couple lay in bed, side-by-side in the dark. They held hands as they peppered their lingering questions with prayers and tears. Around five in the morning, Travis finally drifted to sleep.

Molly lay in the dark, quiet and still. She willed sleep to come, but knew it wouldn't.

At half past six, she slipped out of bed and put on her clothes from the night before. Tiptoeing downstairs, Molly grabbed her keys and headed for the garage. The snow had stopped falling. The streets in her neighborhood were clear. She could safely make it to the main road and to the hospital. Only a few cars were on the streets, probably heading to work.

Molly pulled into the hospital parking lot at 6:40. The main hospital doors would not open until seven. She had two options. She could enter the hospital through the pre-admissions testing department or go around to the back of the building to the emergency room entrance. Molly had been in the pre-admissions department five years ago for her mother's first surgery. To get from there to Laney's room, she would have to weave through corridors to the main hospital.

Molly stared at the pre-admissions door. Her mother had lost her brave fight with cancer. What she wouldn't give to have her mom by her side now. And yet, how grateful she was her mother hadn't lived to see it unfold.

Molly looked at the door and knew she couldn't walk through it. She headed to the back of the building. She could get to Laney's room from the emergency room entrance by taking the back elevators.

A few people were scattered about the waiting room. Molly headed to the elevators. She met several doctors and nurses as she moved through the halls, but no one said anything to her. A large, metal cart laden with breakfast trays was being pushed down the wide corridor.

Molly stood at the door of her daughter's hospital room. Laney was awake. Molly pushed the door open a bit wider, and Laney glanced up. For a moment, Molly thought she caught the trace of a smile on her older child's face.

The smile faded quickly. Laney searched her face. "Rob told you, didn't he?"

Molly rushed in. She wrapped her arms around Laney's shoulders and rocked her daughter. "Everything's going to be okay," Molly said. "You'll see. Everything will be okay."

"I'm so sorry, Mom. I'm so sorry," Laney said. Her voice was quiet.

Molly stroked Laney's hair away from her face. She gently kissed her daughter's forehead. "Oh, Laney."

"It's all my fault," Laney whispered.

"Laney, look at me." Molly held Laney's face in her hands. She bent down to look her daughter square in the eyes. "It was an accident." Her words were slow and deliberate. She tried to speak with authority. The method had worked with Laney as a child and seemed to have a similar calming effect now.

An orderly carried Laney's breakfast into the room and set it on the rolling tray she used as a table, desk, and catchall for her lip balm, comb, and notepad.

Molly slipped into the bathroom and emerged with a warm, wet washcloth for Laney's face. Molly's cell phone rang. Travis.

"I'm okay. I'm with Laney," she spoke into the phone. "If you come to the hospital, I'll buy you a bad cup of coffee."

"Tell him I love him," whispered Laney.

"Laney said to tell you she loves you." Molly handed the phone to Laney.

"I was so mean to you, Daddy," Laney said softly. "I'm so sorry about . . . everything."

Molly smiled. Laney hadn't called Travis "Daddy" in a long time. It was always "Dad" or, since Hunter was born, "Grandpa." So—even if she was numb—her heart was reaching out to them.

The term of endearment wasn't lost on Travis. Within fifteen minutes, he stood by his daughter's side, helping her with her break-fast tray.

Rob called Laney's room around eight o'clock. He apologized for breaking his promise, but Laney assured him all was well. Molly and Travis headed to the cafeteria to give Laney privacy on the phone. On their return, they were surprised to hear a woman say to Laney, "I'm your new best friend."

Chapter 10

MOLLY AND TRAVIS STOOD AT the door of Laney's room, their coffee cups in hand.

"Well, don't jus' stand there. Come on in. I'm Beverly, Miss Laney's liaison."

"Liaison?" Travis looked at the young, black woman seated in a wheelchair in front of him.

"That's right. Liaison. Advocate. She'll be moving to the rehab quad come Monday. That's *my* territory! I was jus' here in the neighborhood—as they say—so I decided to stop by and introduce myself."

Travis moved forward and shook Beverly's extended hand.

Beverly grinned at Laney, jerking her head in Molly's direction. "That your momma? She look jus' like you!"

Before anyone could speak, Beverly started talking again. "Well, I'll be rollin' along now. My kids got swim lessons this afternoon, and I got to drive them since their daddy had to work a double shift. Good to see you already got your copy of the User's Manual. Makes my job a whole lot easier!"

"The user's manual?" Laney asked.

Beverly pointed to the closed book on the corner of the tray table. "The B-I-B-L-E." She turned and began maneuvering her chair toward the door. "I enjoyed meetin' you folks. See you, Laney!" And she was gone.

"She was like a whirlwind," Laney said. "I don't think I got in a word."

"Did she say you're moving Monday?" Molly asked. The imminent move to the rehab unit was a clear sign Laney was getting better.

Laney had already been moved to the rehab unit by the time Rob and Molly arrived Monday morning. An attendant directed them through a maze of hallways to a tunnel connecting the lower level of the hospital to the rehab facility. "The quad," as hospital staff called it, consisted of only four floors, but it was distinctive in design. All offices and medical stations were located on the outside perimeter of the two-story gym, swimming pool, and therapy pools located in the core of the structure.

Laney's new room was on the third floor. By the time Molly and Rob found their way there, Laney had washed up, brushed her teeth, and combed her hair.

"I had to get ready by myself," she said tersely. "Beverly made the personal care aide go away."

Molly looked around the bright room with the big window on the south side. The room itself was much larger than the previous one. On the east wall, a large whiteboard held greetings from the staff scribbled around a detailed schedule.

Molly looked closely. The schedule included a rest time from 2:30 to 4:30 each day, at which time no visitors were allowed. Under the whiteboard was a small chest with a bouquet of flowers on top. "I like your new room."

"It's better than the hospital room." Laney seemed to warm a bit.

"So, who sent the flowers?" Rob asked.

Laney looked puzzled. "I figured they were from you. There wasn't a card. Mom?"

"Not me. Maybe your dad sent them. Or Lissa. All your favorites, just like your wedding bouquet." Molly began poking around the bouquet for an overlooked card.

"You folks have to leave." Molly looked up to see Rob frowning and a hospital attendant pulling Laney's sheet aside. She was all business. "It's time for Mrs. Camden's therapy evaluation."

"I'll get out of your way." Molly moved past the attendant and kissed her daughter on the forehead, leaving Rob behind to deal with the situation.

Hunter and Ellie would have dinner at their grandparents' house during the school week. As she walked through the hospital, she made a mental list of grocery items she needed. She headed to the store to replenish her supply of macaroni and cheese, frozen pizza, and fish sticks. Early on, she had hopes of introducing them to a few new foods, but the fight at dinnertime did not seem worth the effort. Offering one new entree each week became the plan—this week, a nice beef roast with green beans.

Although she wouldn't advertise it, mashed potatoes would be her secret weapon. Surely, she could bribe the children into tasting the roast and some of the green beans with the promise of mashed potatoes as a reward.

Rob put the children on the bus in the mornings, and Molly picked them up every afternoon. On Laney's first three days in rehab, Rob ate dinner with her and had a second dinner with the kids at the Tipton house. Then he or Molly took the kids to see Laney in the rehab unit. Though the now half-hour visits exhausted her, Laney helped Hunter with his homework and listened patiently to Ellie talk on and on about the kindergarten pet hamster.

"Can we have a hamster, Mommy? *Please?*"

"Oh, Ellie, I don't think so," Laney said, looking at Molly. "You'll have to ask Grams about hamsters as pets."

"I don't want a hamster at Gram's house, Mommy," Ellie begged. "I want one at *our* house. And I'll take care of him. I know everything about hamsters."

Hunter sat in the chair, working on his math. "You don't know everything about hamsters."

"I do, too!" Ellie put her hands on her hips, planted her feet in front of him, and leaned in until her face was inches from his. "I know what hamsters eat, and how to clean out their cage, and how to fill the water bottle and everything."

Laney laid her head wearily back on her pillow.

Their time was up anyway. Molly and the children said their goodbyes.

"I hate to say it, Mom," Laney whispered as Molly leaned in to kiss her, "but Ellie and Hunter picking on each other? Somehow, it feels right—normal."

Unconsciously, the family settled into a workable routine. Laney had company scattered throughout the day, instead of everyone huddled in her room all at once. Beverly checked in with Laney daily, usually as she was finishing breakfast and getting ready for her first ninety-minute therapy session.

"That girl of yours is gonna get herself an A on her report card if she keeps up this pace," Beverly told Molly one morning.

Throughout the week, the family learned more about Beverly as well. She had two little girls—Tasha, age five, and Tiara, three. Her husband, Derrick, was a firefighter.

"Derrick was in the military before the accident," Beverly shared. "He didn't have no trouble at all getting on at the fire department."

"Have you always been a patient's advocate?" Laney asked.

"Me? No. Before the accident, I was an aide at the VA hospital in Cincinnati. Course I couldn't do that in a wheelchair. Don't get me wrong; you can do most anything in a wheelchair if you've a mind to; but in my job, I was lifting up those poor, old men and changing the sheets and all."

"Laney was in a car accident," Molly said.

Laney looked up. "Is that what happened to you?"

"No, it was jus' gravity," Beverly replied. "See, my husband was doin' his second tour of duty in Afghanistan, an' I was living by myself on account of all my people live in Georgia. Well, a storm came through, and I had branches scattered all over my roof. I figured Derrick woulda gone up and got those limbs and branches off the roof if he was home, so I decided to do it for him. I climbed up that ladder an' was doing pretty good. Then I picked up a big ol' limb, and it starts going down the backside of the roof, taking me with it. All I needed to do was let go. But I didn't. I guess I thought I could control it or somethin'. Imagine that!" Beverly laughed. "That ol' limb and me went right off the roof. Ten days later, I woke up in the hospital with Derrick right beside me. I lay in that bed for five months. Five months of surgery after surgery before I could start rehab."

"But you have so much energy and such a good attitude."

"Not then I didn't. I felt cheated, madder than a wet hen. But then I started reading my copy of the User's Manual again. I figured God made me, so He could fix me!"

"So did you get mad at God when He didn't—you know—fix you?" Laney asked.

Beverly laughed again. "Well, there's fixing, and there's fixing! And God? Well, He fixed me up jus' the way He wanted to. I learned a whole lot about myself in all that mess. Me? I was holding on to my ol' sinful ways jus' as tight as I had on that branch. You don't let go of sin, and it will pull you down 'til you hit bottom."

Molly eyed her daughter. Was she listening to this or merely acting like it?

"Did you say that was seven years ago?" Molly did the math. "And now you have two little girls?"

Beverly looked straight at Laney and chuckled. "I may be paralyzed, but I'm not dead." Then turning to Molly, she added, "I got more than I ever asked for or expected. That Man Upstairs? He sure knows a whole lot more what's best for me than I do!"

Molly liked this woman. Maybe she could help Laney with more than the physical rehab. In fact, Molly could use a dose of spiritual rehab herself.

Later that evening, Travis fielded two calls. "Lissa called to ask if she could bring a friend home with her for the weekend. I told her that was fine."

"Good. You said there were two calls?"

"Yep." Travis moved behind Molly and put his arms around her as she stuffed the last of the clothes in the washing machine. "Rob said his sister will pick the children up from school this Friday and make dinner for them. We have the night off."

Molly turned and looked at Travis. "Taking care of Hunter and Ellie is a joy. It's not like a job where you need time off! Besides, I was going to make a roast tomorrow."

"I have a better idea. Why don't we go out for dinner? Just the two of us."

Molly leaned her head back into her husband's chest. "We have the whole weekend. Rob's taking the kids to see their great aunt in Columbus on Saturday. She's turning ninety, and the family is having a big party." Rob had balked at going to the birthday party. Laney convinced him to go and take the children.

"Italian or Thai?" Travis asked.

"Thai. The kids would never go with us there!"

Molly busied herself that evening putting fresh linens on the twin beds in what they had always called "the girls' room"—now "Ellie's room." She decided not to worry too much about the guest room, where Hunter slept when he spent the night. She scooted some of Hunter's Legos into a pile in the corner. She didn't want to disrupt whatever it was he was building, but tried to clear a path through so the room at least looked good from the door.

Lissa had never been one to bring friends home from college. Now that she was in graduate school, Molly guessed there was a stronger bond among the smaller core group of students. She was happy Lissa wasn't driving from West Virginia alone.

Everything had worked out great for the weekend. She and Travis would go out to eat on Friday. If she put the roast in the crockpot on Saturday morning, it would be ready when Lissa arrived.

It would be nice to get to know one of Lissa's girlfriends.

Chapter 11

SINCE SHE DIDN'T HAVE TO pick the children up from school, Molly decided to drop by the vocational school on her way to see Laney. If they could work her in, she could get a shampoo and trim in less than thirty minutes. Cassie, a chatty soon-to-be graduate from the beauty college, was the lucky winner to try to transform her from a tired mom and grandma to a beautiful date for Travis.

Cassie eyed her in the mirror as she combed through her hair. "What kind of look are you going for?"

"Make me look younger and thinner."

A little over a half hour later, Molly left feeling—if not younger and thinner—refreshed and happy. She would call the young woman who usually styled Laney's hair to see if she might be interested in making a hospital call.

Walking down the hall, Molly heard garbled voices coming from her daughter's room. She couldn't hear exactly what was being said; but as she moved closer, the room filled with laughter.

Molly pushed the door open. "Lissa! We didn't expect you until tomorrow!"

"I told Dad." Lissa hugged her mother tightly.

"Hmmm. A miscommunication. He told me you were coming only for the weekend."

"Another miscommunication. I'm here for the whole week. It's spring break."

"The whole week? That's wonderful!"

"Uh, Mom, did Dad tell you I was bringing a friend?"

"That part he got right."

"Good." Lissa motioned to the tall man now standing slightly behind Molly. "Mom, this is my friend, Mark. Mark, this is my mom."

"I am so pleased to meet you, Mrs. Tipton. Melissa has told me all about you," he said from behind a beard.

A man? This was Lissa's friend? Molly tried to hold her smile steady. "We have heard so much about you, too" would be an outright lie. "I'm pleased to meet you as well, Mark. I really appreciate you driving Lissa here."

"Mark is in the same department I am in at WVU, but we met in church," Lissa said. "I told him we have room in the guest room, right?"

Molly nodded and smiled. She really needed to call Travis and change their plans. Not only did she need to rethink dinner, she needed desperately to get home and clean Hunter's room.

"You look different, Mom. Did you get your hair done?" Laney asked.

Molly touched her hair, feeling a little foolish. "I needed a little trim. Look, I'm going to head out of here, and I'll see you at home, okay? Dinner at six?"

Molly kissed her girls and left the room. Only a few steps down the hall, she called Travis.

"Her friend is a man with a beard named Mark. And I guess our dinner plans are off."

"Why don't they just come with us?" Travis suggested.

Molly was about to nix the idea when she boarded the elevator and got cut off. The ride down to the lobby gave her a minute to think.

"Okay," she said to Travis once they had reconnected. "We'll take them out for Italian. If I don't have to cook, it will give me time to clean Hunter's room; but the Thai food is our special date night food, agreed?"

"Agreed." Molly could almost hear her husband's smile over the phone.

Molly and Travis took Lissa and Mark to Enrico's. Mark waved off the recommendation for their specialty spaghetti with a laugh. "I don't think spaghetti and this beard are a good combination for a 'meet the parents' kind of dinner."

So that's what this is. A "meet the parents dinner." Her mind raced. How long had Lissa known this man? Why hadn't they heard anything about him? Why was Travis laughing and joking without any thought being given to the "meet the parents" comment? Was he that thick-headed? Molly wanted to grab her younger daughter by the hand and take her somewhere where the two of them could talk.

Instead, she ordered lasagna and a dinner salad.

"Mom!"

"I just wondered how serious this relationship is."

Travis and Mark were playing a video game in the "man cave." With the men safely out of earshot, Molly was able to finally get the story behind Lissa's "friend."

"Like I said, Mom, we're friends. Good friends."

"How good?"

Lissa was the one grinning now. "He's the nicest man I have ever met. He's generous and kind. And he's smart. I was going to tell you about him; but then when everything happened with Laney, I just figured it could wait."

Molly stroked her daughter's chestnut brown hair, thinking of the time an invitation to the senior class honors ceremony arrived in the mail. *"Oh, yeah,"* Lissa had said in that same tone of voice, *"I was going to tell you I got a scholarship; but with Laney's wedding and all, I just figured it could wait."*

Later that night, as he and Molly prepared for bed, Travis said, "I like him."

Molly fluffed her pillow. "Lissa is pretty fond of him herself. I wouldn't be surprised if they announce an engagement soon."

Travis wrinkled his forehead. "Do you really think so?"

Molly shook her head. "You don't think he's just some nice guy who drove Lissa home for spring break, do you?"

"No, but . . . " Travis looked lost.

"Travis. Really. Face the facts, buddy. Your baby girl is all grown up."

Mark was staying only through Sunday and returning the following weekend. Travis awoke early Saturday morning and made French toast. Lissa laid out her plan to show Mark around town and take lunch to Laney.

"I wish Rob and the kids were around," Lissa said. "I wanted Mark to meet them."

Lissa and Mark decided to take church to Laney Sunday morning. Molly started to say she wasn't sure how well-received their efforts would be but let it go.

The days and weeks since the accident had drained the Tipton household like an endless, bleak winter. The paper February calendar, with its penciled-in *Pick up Hunter* on that fateful Friday looked tired and old. Lissa, like spring, brought energy and new life to the house. Now, as they entered the first full week in March, Lissa pulled down the old calendar and made a notation on the new one.

"Anniversary dinner," Molly read. "I hadn't even thought about our anniversary!"

"You and Dad are going out."

Laney insisted they come by the hospital on their way to the restaurant. "And wear make-up, Mom!"

Molly felt as though she were on a prom date, modeling her new gown for the parents. Only her "gown" was a pair of dress slacks and a soft, white sweater with a sequined collar.

"Have her home early!" Lissa called after them as they left Laney's room.

An hour later, at their favorite place, Travis handed the server his menu. "I always look at the whole menu and think I should try something new, but I always come back to the Chicken Pad Thai."

"Sometimes, it's good to just stay with something you know you like."

Travis grinned. "Is that why you've kept me around all these years?"

"Yep." Molly looked into her husband's eyes. There, she found the same boy she fell in love with those many years ago.

Mark's arrival on Friday evening marked Lissa's imminent departure to West Virginia. She'd spent every day with Laney and every afternoon with the kids.

"I've loved going to therapy with Laney," Lissa told Molly as they prepared Sunday's breakfast. "I keep thinking there must be mechanical solutions to help Laney."

"That's the engineer in you talking."

"I know. I have a notebook full of questions to research when I get back to school."

The tempo of the contemporary service worship band seemed to mirror the pounding of Molly's heart. Ever since the accident, she and Travis had been attending the early, more traditional service, but Lissa wanted to reconnect with her friends.

Rob brought the children to church. Was it to see Lissa or to check out Mark? It didn't matter. Molly's heart was filled with joy. *If only Laney were here.*

A young man walked up to the platform, a guitar in hand. Words to "A Mighty Fortress" appeared on the screen at the front of the auditorium. This rendition of the song wasn't the heavy, organ-dominated version they'd sung in the traditional service a few weeks earlier. The intricate patterns of the guitar carried a message of human weakness and God's power.

Molly found herself listening more closely to the words, lingering here and there on a particular phrase. "He amid the flood / Of mortal ills prevailing . . . " *That's us. A flood of mortal ills. Sometimes, I feel like I'm coming undone, Lord.*

Pastor Haynes stood to deliver the sermon, which he now called a message. Molly opened her bulletin to retrieve the outline, called "Beyond Temptation." If only Laney hadn't given in to the temptation of alcohol.

Lissa and Mark wrote down everything Pastor Haynes said. Was she missing something?

Though they hoped to leave early enough to navigate the winding West Virginia roads before dark, Lissa and Mark lingered, visiting with Lissa's church friends for a while in the church's large atrium.

"Mrs. Tipton?" Molly turned to see Andrea standing with two young children in tow, a man beside her. "You remember my husband, Evan?"

"Evan." Molly extended her hand. *Had Laney called Andrea? No, that didn't make sense.*

"We've been coming to church the past two weeks," Andrea shared. "After what happened to Tori and Laney, we figure life can be sort of—I don't know—fragile, I guess. We didn't have a church, and I remembered coming here once with Laney. I hope it's okay."

Was she asking permission to come to church?

Molly put on what she hoped was her most gracious smile. "Of course."

"We like it a lot. I went to church as a kid, but nothing like this," Evan said.

"Anyway, I saw you standing here and wanted to say hi," Andrea said.

Andrea was about to leave, when Lissa turned her way. "Andrea?"

"Liss? When did you get back in town?"

Lissa and Andrea hugged each other like old friends. Lissa chattered about spring break while guiding Andrea, Evan, and their children toward the main door where Mark, Rob, and Travis seemed to be in deep conversation. Rob shook Evan's hand with a welcoming smile.

Molly stood watching. She'd had no clue they knew each other so well. Even Travis looked comfortable with the crowd. They were all laughing and talking as if everything in the world was just right. Here she stood, holding Hunter's jacket and Ellie's heavy, hooded coat while everyone else seemed to be having a grand, old time.

Why do I feel jealous about this, Lord? I should be happy Andrea and Evan are here.

Ellie ran to her side. "Look, Grams! I made a tree with my hand-print. Did you know even the trees praise God?"

"That's right, Ellie; even the trees clap their hands and praise God."

Saying goodbye to Lissa in the church parking lot left Molly feeling sullen and empty. Rob left with Hunter and Ellie to spend the day with Laney, planning to pick up Happy Meals on the way. "I need a Happy Meal, too," Molly said to no one in particular.

"What?" asked Travis.

"Nothing. Just thinking."

As they drove home, Molly turned her face toward the window. She didn't want to tell Travis what she was feeling. Somehow, the whole scene at church was unsettling. Everyone else's life went on while her precious daughter lay paralyzed in the hospital. She was the only one who cared about Laney—the only one unwilling to betray her. They should all be miserable right now.

And what was it with Andrea?

But then, what had Andrea really done? Survived? Acted responsibly? Sought to bring her children to church?

Molly had only halfway listened to the sermon. Yet there was an impression left on her. A loosely formed thought, just out of her reach. Something about temptation. Not Laney's. More like her own. Temptation to lay the blame for all of their woes at somebody's feet. Tori's? Andrea's?

Anybody but Laney.

Chapter 12

WINTER WOULDN'T YIELD OFFICIALLY TO spring for another week, but the temperature Monday morning was unusually warm. Molly and Travis gave in to the invitation, carrying their morning coffee out onto the deck. The furniture with its brightly colored cushions was still stowed away in the basement, so the two leaned against the deck railing, sipping their coffee and listening to the cardinals and finches.

"Feeling better?" Travis inquired.

Molly nodded. "Sorry I was a bit down yesterday."

"That's okay. We're all under attack these days."

Molly studied her husband's face. What did he mean? Laney was the one who had been attacked. Satan had used Tori and Andrea to pull Laney into a pit of destruction, never to walk again.

Destruction. That was one of the words in yesterday's sermon. Antagonism toward Andrea began creeping back.

"I've been thinking a lot about the sermon yesterday." Travis interrupted her evil thoughts. "I have to admit that ever since the accident, I've been easily distracted from my own Bible study. I mean, I feel like I'm praying all the time for Laney, but I haven't been arming myself with God's Word like the pastor said yesterday. It's like when you don't feed yourself the right foods, you get sick. And then once you get sick, you're vulnerable to all kinds of other viruses and stuff. You know what I mean?"

"Uh-huh." Molly nodded, taking a sip of her coffee. She vaguely remembered something about Satan trying to distract and destroy Jesus. She knew the story about how he'd taken Jesus up to the mountain to tempt Him. Again, she had tuned out what the pastor was saying because she thought she already knew. The parts she *did* listen to, she applied to everyone but herself.

Later that morning, Molly called the church office to order a CD of the worship service. She needed to listen to the message this time without thinking about everything and everyone else.

Laney was already dressed and in her wheelchair when Molly arrived. Ellie's picture from Sunday school was taped to the wall. A large vase held a bouquet of purple and yellow irises. Their sweet fragrance filled the small room.

"Aren't those beautiful?" Laney sounded happy. "A woman from work brought them from her garden."

"They are gorgeous. My irises are not even close to blooming yet. By the way, did you ever ask Lissa about those flowers without the card?"

"I asked her the night they came. She didn't send them. She's still 'technically a college student with no flower money.'"

"Huh. I wonder who sent them."

"I don't know, but Lissa said we can give her credit since they were so beautiful." Laney grinned.

Talk was easy today—about Hunter's new desire to join the swim team and Ellie trying to roll around in Laney's wheelchair. They talked about the picture Ellie had made.

"Ellie told me she was bringing me church just like Aunt Lissa did. She said the trees clap their hands. That's in the Bible, isn't it? I remember we used to sing a song about it in youth group."

"I know it's in the Bible, but I don't remember where exactly."

Molly busied herself straightening Laney's side table. "Oh, did I tell you Andrea and Evan were at church? I guess they've been coming to the second service." Laney's Bible was still on the table. Had she opened it lately?

Have I?

"I tried so hard to get Andrea to come with me to church when we were in college," Laney said. "She came to see me last week, but never mentioned church."

It was Molly's turn to be surprised. She didn't realize her daughter had ever invited Andrea—or anyone else, for that matter—to attend church with her. *I wonder if she ever asked Tori.* No need to go there now. *Change the subject.*

"So, what do you think of Mark?" Molly asked.

"I like him. He's a good fit for Lissa. And the whole family."

"So, you think it's serious?"

"Mom, get real. How many times have you known Lissa to ever bring a guy home just to meet you and Dad?"

"Point taken."

"Besides, we talk every night. She's told me all about him. He's the one. You can count on it."

Molly wouldn't get the CD from church until the following Sunday, so she rummaged through Travis' music collection until she found a contemporary remake of traditional hymns to play in her car. "A Mighty Fortress" was near the top of the list. The strains of music washed over her on her way to work.

During Sunday's sermon, Molly had latched onto the thought of "our ancient foe." Satan was, indeed, crafty. On Sunday, she had allowed her thoughts to label Tori and Andrea as agents of the Evil One.

Now as she listened, she heard a message of hope against all trials. God never fails; but when we rely on our own strength, we lose. On Sunday, Molly had wondered why this song, with its cumbersome language, had been chosen for the contemporary service. Today, she knew. It was for her.

Wednesday afternoon, Molly dropped by just after Laney's therapy session. She found Rob standing at the foot of Laney's bed, his hands on his head.

"Go away! Leave!" Laney screamed.

Molly rushed to Laney's side. "What's wrong? What happened?"

"Get out!" she screamed at her mother. "Go away!"

Beverly accompanied the two of them as they retreated to the waiting area. "Nothin' new here. She's not depressed, jus' a little discouraged. She jus' started learnin' stuff like bladder management and bowel care. It hit her, that's all."

"What 'hit her'?" Molly asked.

Beverly gently touched Molly's arm. "This is for real. This isn't gonna go away. 'Til now, Miss Laney in there been thinking that, somehow, this is one big mistake. That, somehow, she's gonna be different. But you start talking about takin' care of yourself, your bladder and all, and it hits you!"

A lump formed in Molly's throat.

"She's gonna be all right. You'll see. Give her a little time."

All the way home, Molly gripped the steering wheel. Her shoulders and neck drew tight with tension, and her head began to ache. Hadn't she herself questioned the reality of the paralysis? Laney complained early on that her legs hurt. The doctor called them phantom pains. Laney's brain was playing a cruel trick.

The doctor had said, "She *may* never walk again." *May.* Laney had always latched onto such words growing up. *I said we* may *go to the park after lunch, Laney.* Or *Daddy said* maybe *we would get a puppy.*

How many times had Molly and Travis given in to her begging? How many times had they confirmed that *may* or *maybe* meant *yes?* Hobo—the terrier who had occupied their home and taken up residence in their hearts for fourteen years—was evidence of a *maybe* turning into a *yes.* Once she had moved into the rehab unit, Laney must have convinced herself the paralysis was temporary.

Now she had to face the truth.

A staff counselor met with Laney and Rob both one-on-one and together. "Rob really needs our support right now," Travis told Molly.

"They both do," Molly argued.

"Laney is going to be okay. Watch. She'll throw herself into being the best paraplegic on earth, but it's hard on a man to see his wife go through something like this. Harder than going through it himself."

Molly's thoughts flew to her mother's bedside. "It's harder on you," her mother had whispered. "Always harder on the people beside the bed than the one in it."

Travis was right. By the weekend, Laney was reading everything she could find on life as a paraplegic. She was determined to tackle this head on.

Evelyn Starks, a woman in her fifties, was assigned as Laney's social worker. She wanted to meet with Rob and Laney to discuss Laney's progress.

"Rob and I want you and Dad to be there," Laney said on the phone. "She's coming today at two o'clock. I know it's short notice, but we would really appreciate it."

She and Travis arrived a few minutes before two, though Molly didn't look forward to it. She had met the cold, solemn Ms. Starks once before, concerning an insurance matter.

"Well, how is our star patient? I hear you've been working very hard," Ms. Starks began. The words may have been intended to sound friendly, but the woman spoke without emotion. In her dark blue suit, she came off more like a prison guard than a businesswoman. Her dark hair was cropped close to her head, short and shapeless.

There were only three chairs in the room, so Travis leaned against the side of Laney's bed. Ms. Starks cast a stern look at him. Travis shifted his weight.

"It's never too early to think about where you go from here. In a few weeks, you will be dismissed, so we need to start thinking about where we'll send you." She made it sound like Laney was some product of the hospital to be shipped out.

"I can go home?" Laney's voice was full of hope.

Molly pressed her lips together to hold in her sigh. All Laney had heard was "dismissed."

"Maybe. We'll see." There it was. *Maybe.* Ms. Starks should have given up then. Laney was going home. "First, we'll check into a long-term care facility."

A warehouse. Molly had investigated a few such facilities when her mother was ill. Some were excellent. Unfortunately, the ones her mother's insurance covered were less than stellar. In the end, Molly's mother came to live with her and Travis right up until the end of her life. It was the right decision.

"What will it take to bring her home?" Rob asked.

"I doubt you realize the challenges you'd face. Don't you have two young children? And most homes are ill-fitted to meet the demands of someone assigned to a wheelchair."

"If she can be released medically, I'll figure out the rest," Rob persisted.

"We will do anything and everything we need to do," volunteered Travis. Molly nodded in full agreement. There was no way she was sending her daughter off to a "facility."

Ms. Starks looked at the resolved faces before her. A smile, sincere and warm, crept across her face. "That's what I like to hear. Laney, you have a strong family, and that's half the battle. Your determination is the other half."

"Quarter," said a voice from the doorway. Beverly wheeled herself through the opening. "Gotta give God at least seventy-five percent; then you are free to divide up the rest any way you want."

Laney rolled her eyes. "Funny, I would have expected you to say God is one hundred percent."

"Right! He is!"

Ms. Starks handed Rob a checklist with which they could evaluate the Camden home for accessibility, mobility, and meeting daily needs.

"There are a few support groups who can help you evaluate the house, though not much by way of an organized effort here in Cincinnati. I'll try to get a list together."

"No need. Already done." Beverly was the poster child for taking initiative.

"What about a van or something?" Molly inquired.

Ms. Starks assumed her former stern-faced self. She scowled at Molly. "Mrs. Camden is hardly ready to drive yet."

"I mean for getting her home, going places," Molly stammered. Why did she feel so awkward around this woman?

As Travis walked Molly out to her car a few minutes later, Molly shook her head. "That woman is so scary!"

"She's just sort of brash," Travis said.

"For being in the people business, she sure lacks people skills."

"She's probably developed a thick skin doing this every day."

"Don't make excuses for her, Travis. She's annoying."

"Annoying but efficient."

"Yeah, well, I prefer nice and efficient."

Travis opened Molly's car door for her. "Not everyone can be like you." He kissed her on the cheek. "Listen, I'm heading back to work. You and Rob and I will sit down and figure this out after dinner." Beverly had suggested they not only use the list, but also sit in various places in the rooms to see the space from Laney's perspective.

Molly pulled out of the hospital parking lot. She had an even better idea.

Chapter 13

LINDEN LANE COMMUNITY CHURCH REFERRED to a collection of crutches, walkers, portable bedside commodes, and wheelchairs as their "medical ministry." Members of the church could check out supplies as needed.

Kate, the church secretary, unlocked the storage room. "Are you getting the wheelchair for Laney?"

"Sort of." Molly looked over the three available chairs. Only one looked to be about the right size. It was covered in a layer of dust.

"Just needs a little soap and water," Kate said. "We've all been praying for Laney. Did you know the girl who died?"

"Yes." The word caught in her throat. Usually people avoided discussion of Tori.

Molly sat down in the dusty chair and closed her eyes.

Kate rolled a wide, green wheelchair across from her and sat down.

"Tori was an old friend of Laney's from college," Molly began. "She was in town; so Laney, Tori, and another friend got together. Laney was driving Tori back to where she was staying when they had the accident. She knows Tori died, but she doesn't remember the accident."

Kate reached for Molly's hand. "Maybe that's a blessing. I think sometimes God just protects us from remembering bad things."

"The weather was bad that night; but to make matters worse, Laney and her friend had been to a bar. The sheriff didn't charge her with a DUI, but alcohol was a contributor." Molly hadn't expected to confess this.

"Stuff like that happens, Molly. Nobody's perfect." Kate didn't act any differently knowing Laney had been drinking. Kate pulled Molly to her feet and wrapped her arms around her. She began to pray.

"Dear Heavenly Father," Kate whispered. "I praise You for the way You're healing our sweet Laney. I praise You for the strength You're giving Molly and Travis and Melissa and the way You're helping Rob and the kids.

"And I want to pray for Tori's family. Comfort them, Lord. And I know a wound can't heal until it's all aired out, Lord, so thank You for helping Molly do that. In the name of Jesus, amen."

Molly allowed the tears to stream down her cheeks. The two women held each other for several minutes.

"Thank you," Molly whispered.

Eventually, Kate and Molly wrestled the wheelchair out from the tangle of stored goods, up the stairs, and out to the car. They struggled for a few minutes figuring out how to fold the metal contraption to a more manageable size before sliding it into the empty trunk space.

"Is there anything else you need?" Kate asked.

"Actually, yes. I ordered a CD . . . "

"I have it on my desk. I'll get it for you."

Molly would be late picking up Ellie from the sitter. The meeting with Ms. Starks had lasted only twenty-five minutes, but what Molly intended to be a short trip to church had turned into forty minutes of intense, freeing confession and prayer. She fished for her cell phone.

"Jenny? Molly Tipton. I'm on my way." She heard a child scream, followed by crying. "Jenny?"

"Hold on, Molly." Jenny had two children of her own and another kindergartner named Alex there for the afternoon. Alex was a little rough.

"Sorry about that, Molly. Alex and Ellie got in a fight over the game they were playing."

"Is she okay?"

"Ellie's fine. Alex was the one crying. Don't worry; everything's under control."

Had it always been this hard? She couldn't remember her children getting in fights where others were hurt and crying. Then again, maybe this was like what Kate said about remembering painful incidents. Maybe her children fought. Maybe God just blessed her with a happy lapse in memory.

Though nothing was said about Alex, Ellie chattered all the way home from the sitter's house. "I want to get a hamster. Mommy said you could tell me all about house hamsters."

Molly smiled to herself. Laney, who dearly loved her own pet as a child, now saw the issue with the eyes of a parent. The last thing anyone in the Camden household needed right now was a hamster.

What could she tell her granddaughter? "The simple truth is, hamsters aren't very good house pets. We tried it once, and our hamster kept escaping from his cage. I changed his name to Houdini."

"What's a Houdini?"

Molly told her granddaughter about the famous escape artist. She really didn't know much but managed to recount enough about magic tricks to intrigue Ellie. For the remainder of the ride, Ellie didn't mention the hamster.

Rob and Laney would be the ones to tell the kids about Laney coming home, so Molly didn't say anything. When Hunter got off the bus, she told them they could play for a while.

"We're eating here tonight as soon as your dad and grandpa get home from work."

"Yippee!" Hunter cried as he raced to his own bedroom.

"You would have thought it was Christmas," Molly told Travis when he arrived.

"So, did you get to work on the report you brought home?" Travis busied himself trying to fix the head of one of Ellie's Barbie dolls.

"I didn't even take it out of the car. I was late to pick up Ellie, and then I cleaned the refrigerator and ran a load of laundry." Molly cleared the kitchen table of schoolwork, Sunday's newspaper, and an assortment of matchbox cars. She pulled plates from the cabinet.

Rob was bringing a special dinner home. She finished setting the table when he walked through the door carrying a bucket of fried chicken with double sides of macaroni and cheese.

"I figured it was about time I cooked for you!" There was a definite bounce in his step. He leaned in and whispered, "We're going to wait to tell the kids after the doc gives us a more definitive date."

"Just the fact they are using words like 'dismissal' and 'home' . . . " Molly whispered back.

During dinner, Ellie brought up the pet hamster again, pestering Rob this time. None of his arguments convinced her to drop the issue. Exasperated, Rob sighed. "Look. Mommy's coming home, and she needs rest. She doesn't need a hamster around."

"Mommy's coming home?" Hunter jumped up, knocking over his chair.

Ellie squealed. "When?"

Both jumped and danced around the table. "Mommy's coming home! Mommy's coming home!"

Travis raised his eyebrows and looked at Molly. "So much for waiting."

It took all three adults to explain that they weren't sure when Laney would come home. Molly suggested the children could help get the house ready by cleaning their bedrooms.

Both kids raced upstairs and were soon throwing toys in their toy boxes. While they worked, Travis and Rob looked over the checklist. Molly went out to the garage to retrieve the wheelchair.

"I got this at church. I thought we could sit in it and see everything from Laney's perspective like Beverly said." Molly sat down in the blue vinyl seat. "Hmmm . . . It's the same view as in any chair." Molly moved the wheels to propel her forward. *Awkward.*

Moving on the kitchen floor was doable, but the counter and island were immense roadblocks. At the edge of the living room, the wheels caught on the carpet.

"So far, this house stinks!" Rob announced. "I knew we would have to build a ramp or something so she could get in, but this? Laney and I talked today about moving our bedroom down here to the dining room. We have a half-bath on this level, so that helps."

Molly wheeled toward the half-bath. No way could she get in there. "The wheels don't fit. Besides that, even if she got in, what if she needed help? Nobody else could get in to help her."

Travis chewed his lip. "I think we should contact Evan. He's a contractor. Maybe he could help us figure out what to do."

"Evan?" asked Molly.

"Andrea's husband."

Rob scratched his head. "That's a great idea, Travis, but where are we going to get the money for those kinds of renovations?"

"We can save money by doing some of the work ourselves." Travis looked at Molly. "And we have some savings."

"And a lot of friends have offered to help any way they can," Molly added. "I'm sure we have a ton of talent at church willing to do whatever we need."

"Do you really think they would help?" asked Rob. "I mean, with everything that happened and all . . . "

"Just call Evan and see if he has any ideas," Travis instructed. "And don't worry about the front deck and ramp. I can build that myself. Just get his ideas on renovating this part of the house and an estimate."

Rob reached for the phone and made arrangements for Evan to meet him the following afternoon.

That evening on the phone, Lissa cautioned her mother. "Just make sure you get Laney in on the plans. You don't want to tear up a woman's house without consulting her first."

"We're doing only stuff that has to be done." She breathed deeply. "But, yeah, we'll talk it over with Laney."

The Camden house was 102 years old when Laney and Rob had found it almost six years ago. They had started the search as soon as Laney discovered she was pregnant with Ellie. Their apartment had been a tight squeeze when Hunter came along—definitely no room for a second child. The house on Mercedes Avenue was old but in their price range.

Rob had been reluctant. Laney loved it. The neighborhood—old and established—was beautiful. The high ceilings and original woodwork held appeal for Laney. The fact the previous owners had replaced the windows and updated the electric, furnace, and plumbing pleased Rob. The three bedrooms were upstairs. That would be a problem now.

Evan, Andrea, Molly, Travis, Rob, and Laney met in Laney's room on Saturday.

"Evan has stayed up late every night researching adaptive and universal design plans. And he talks about it constantly," Andrea shared. "He says remodeling a space to meet the needs of someone with a disability is intriguing."

Disability? Molly cringed at the word.

Evan pulled up the plans on his computer and projected them on the wall for all to see. "There's more to universal design than just widening the doors and making it easy for the wheelchair to move. We'll need to move electrical sockets up a bit and light switches down some to make each more accessible for Laney."

Evan began the slide show presentation from his laptop. Computer generated drawings displayed on the wall helped Molly envision the space as Evan designed it. He described the details.

The estimate Evan quoted was twenty thousand more than Travis expected, even allowing for volunteer help and donating his own time as job foreman. There was just no way to avoid the costs of the bathroom and kitchen renovation. One change led to another—cabinets, load-bearing walls, new beams, new wiring. Everything.

"Do you know anything about the condition of the subflooring?" Evan asked Rob.

"Nothing. The carpet was new when we moved in."

"I like the idea of an open concept and laminate floors," Laney said.

Evan traced the lines of the new kitchen counter and the new island separating the kitchen from the living room. "All of these spaces, including the island, have countertops at your level. I made sure you could reach the electrical outlets and everything."

Laney used Evan's laser pointer. "Is this a closet?"

"Yes, with a dressing room. You can enter it from the bedroom or the bathroom."

"So, what happened to the washer and dryer?" Rob asked.

Evan pointed to a closet in the bathroom. "They're still here, just behind these pocket doors. Pocket doors won't get in Laney's way. And we'll need to replace the existing appliances with front loading ones like these." Evan pulled up a picture of a washer and dryer on his computer screen. He pointed out the control panel located on the front.

Travis and Rob looked at each other. Rob knew the cost was more than either of them anticipated. Molly and Travis had a separate savings set aside. They had hoped to move to Florida during the winter months when they retired.

Laney liked the look of the new face on her old house.

Molly wanted Laney to be happy. She nodded to Travis.

"When can you start?" Travis asked.

Chapter 14

REMODELING THE CAMDEN HOUSE REQUIRED removing everything from the main level. Rob and the children moved in with the Tiptons for the duration.

Molly packed items from the kitchen cabinets into boxes and carried them to the basement, along with the furniture Travis and Rob hauled down. The men made room for the sofa in the garage.

The antique dining room furniture that had once been Molly's grandmother's was a bit trickier. Travis and Rob loaded the large pieces in the back of a rental truck and took them to the Tipton house, where they put everything in the seldom-used formal living room. Molly and Travis now had wall-to-wall furniture in the small space.

Three of Travis's friends from the men's prayer breakfast group arrived at the Camden house after dinner the following evening to pull up all of the carpet and the linoleum in the kitchen.

Once back at the Tipton house, Rob headed straight for the shower. Travis, dirty and tired, pulled a stack of cookies from a box in the pantry. "There were hardwood floors under all that carpet and linoleum. They're scuffed and dull, but seem to be solid. Evan says that by refinishing the existing floors, we'll save a good three thousand dollars."

Travis and Rob worked evenings and all day Saturday on the house. Molly turned into the gofer. As long as Evan and his team came through on time, Laney would come home by Easter to a house fitted for her.

Sunday would be a welcomed day of rest. Last Sunday's message on CD lay unopened in its plastic case on the front seat of Molly's car. Now, it was time for a new sermon.

Pastor Haynes had everyone stand and read the Lord's Prayer together. Molly recited it from memory.

"Many of us memorized that prayer as children," Pastor Haynes said. "But how many of us think about what prayer means in our lives today?"

Busted. Molly's shoulders felt the weight of her own pride. *I act like I have it all together, but I'm a mess.* When, in the last week, had she prayed a real prayer, not one of those "canned versions" she recited with all of the religious-sounding words? How long had it been since she talked *with* God and not *at* Him? She had prayed *for* Laney, but she hadn't prayed *with* Laney.

"And forgive us our debts as we also forgive our debtors," Pastor Haynes read. "Let's examine that."

Let's not. Church hadn't been all that comfortable lately. She forced herself to focus on the remainder of the service.

"Prayer is one of those tools Jesus used to keep the Evil One at bay," Pastor Haynes said.

Eventually, the message ended, but Molly found herself wanting more.

With Rob and the kids at the hospital and Travis in his man-cave, Molly fixed herself a cup of tea, retrieved the CD from her car, and put it into the player in the family room. Settling into Travis' soft, leather recliner, Molly closed her eyes to listen.

Pastor Haynes' voice boomed through the speaker, delivering the message he called, "Beyond Temptation." The recorded sermon centered on Satan tempting Jesus to deny his Father. "Notice Satan's timing. He waits until Jesus is vulnerable," Pastor Haynes said. "That's what he does with us. He waits until we are at our weakest point. And how did Jesus respond each time? He quoted Scripture. We need to steep ourselves in Scripture."

Molly had made a New Year's resolution to read through the Bible during the calendar year. She'd tried a few years earlier but failed. This time, she had worked her way through Genesis and Exodus before giving up.

"Steeping" in the Scripture sounded a far cry from simply reading through it. Molly often couldn't remember what she had read. She read to get through the chapters and put a checkmark in the box. She took a sip of tea. "Steeped in Scripture. Soaking in God's Word," Molly said out loud.

The radio alarm clock, set for 6:00 a.m., sounded with "I Got You Babe." It reminded Molly of *Groundhog Day*. What would happen if Laney had the chance to relive that horrible Friday over and over until she changed her life? Molly lay in bed pondering the possibilities as Travis got ready for work.

If I could change the events of today, what would I do?

"Interesting," she said out loud.

"What's interesting?" Travis buttoned his shirt.

"I was thinking about that movie *Groundhog Day*. Do you remember it?"

"Yeah, I think so. The guy kept waking up to the same day, right? And then he started using that to his advantage. What made you think of that?"

Molly sat up in the bed, watching her husband select a pair of socks from the drawer. "A song. But what I was thinking was how every decision we make from the minute we get out of bed shapes our day."

"Profound."

"That sounded sarcastic."

Travis leaned in to kiss his wife. "Sorry, I guess I didn't watch the movie with your philosophical eye. My first decision today is to go to work. I have a breakfast meeting with our staff."

Travis headed downstairs as Molly fell back on her pillow. *Lord, today I want to make deliberate decisions based on what You want, not on what I want. Please.*

Molly didn't want to move. Once she got up and into her day, she might lose this insight God had revealed to her. Wasn't there a song that said something like "take the way I feel at this moment and seal my heart right now for Heaven"? She lay in the bed as long as she could, but finally had to get moving.

Travis didn't need her to cook breakfast. Rob and the kids were already gone. The house was quiet. Molly decided to get ready first, forego her dose of daily news, and read her Bible instead.

She hummed in the shower. The tune was familiar, but she struggled to remember the words. As she worked the shampoo into her hair, they flooded her mind. "Come, thou Fount of every blessing, tune my heart to sing thy grace; streams of mercy, never ceasing, call for songs of loudest praise." *That's it. That's the song about sealing my heart.*

Uncertain of the verses, she hummed a bit, filling in words when they came to her. "Hmmm . . . Jesus sought me when a stranger, wandering from the fold of God; He, to rescue me from danger . . . hmmm . . . His precious blood."

The words she sought were near as she hummed her way into the final verse. By now, the shampoo trailed down her face and neck. "Prone to wander, Lord, I feel it, prone to leave the God I love; here's my heart, O take and seal it; seal it for thy courts above."

Laney was dressed and eating breakfast when her mother arrived. "Good morning! Wow, you're eating oatmeal? I couldn't get you to even try it."

"Yeah, well, I met with the nutritionist on Friday. Actually, with a little brown sugar and pecans, it's pretty good."

Molly sat down in the chair. She wanted to share her experience this morning and maybe even pray with her daughter. No. If she did that, she would have to admit that up until now, she had just been going through the motions of being a Christian. Laney would roll her eyes and call her a hypocrite.

"Well, look who's here!" Beverly's voice boomed from the doorway. "I saw you come in, so I brought you a cup of coffee."

"Thanks." Molly reached for the cup. "So, how's our girl doing?"

"Couple weeks and Miss Laney here will be ready to go. She's strong, and she's a hard worker. Already got all the transfers down. She can dress herself and take care of herself jus' fine. Today, we gonna be cooking and doing laundry."

Laney tilted her head. "Life Skills class. In fact, if all goes well, I'm surprising Rob with dinner."

"Meatloaf and mashed potatoes. It don't get much better than that!"

"No mac and cheese?"

Laney shot Molly a frown. "Mac and cheese is for babies. I'm going for box-free cooking."

"I think that would be called 'cooking from scratch.'" Molly smiled.

"Whatever. It's meatloaf and mashed potatoes today and then onward and upward."

"Well, don't get too excited," Beverly advised. "I'm your coach on this job, an' I only got me one or two sure-fire recipes."

A couple of weeks. If they were going to have the house ready for Laney's homecoming, they needed to shift the work into high gear. Evan's crew was busy now that all of the permits had cleared. Travis would build the access ramps himself.

With the work in full swing, Molly and Ellie could no longer wait at the house for Hunter's bus. Instead, she picked Hunter up at school first, leaving Ellie with the sitter to be collected on her way home.

Today, Molly was anxious to get Hunter and Ellie home. She arrived at Hunter's school in time to see him saunter through the glass doors. "Hi, Grams!" He chatted about his super day all the way to pick up Ellie.

Ellie was a different story. She begged to stay at Jenny's. She couldn't find her shoes, then whined during the ride home. By the time Molly reached her house, she was exhausted. Ellie, though, getting her second wind, was fighting with Hunter.

Rob called to say he was eating a dinner Laney cooked for him that day. Now if only she could get Ellie in a better frame of mind. She tried everything. Ellie cheered up only when Rob arrived.

Rob swooped Ellie up in his arms and kissed her on both cheeks. "How's Daddy's girl?"

"I'm Grandpa's girl."

"Is that so? Well, you can be Grandpa's girl and my girl, too, you know."

"Can I have a hamster?"

"No."

"Then I am just going to be Grandpa's girl."

Rob lowered Ellie to the floor. "Your choice." Then turning to Molly, he said, "Travis isn't siding with her on the hamster, is he?"

"He better not! So, tell me about your dinner."

Rob described the Dubois Family Life Center located on the rehab unit. "They have a living area set up like a typical living room, a kitchen, bathroom, and bedroom right there in the unit."

"Is it—what's the word Evan calls it? Universal design?"

"No, it's your regular stuff. Setting the oven dial was hard. It'll be easier for her with Evan's design."

Molly finished cleaning up the dishes. She took so much for granted. Turn on the oven? Easy. Stand here washing dishes? No problem. In fact, washing the dishes by hand was satisfying.

After the children were in bed, the men sat at the kitchen table making a new to-do list. Molly divided her time between a load of laundry and staying in on the conversation.

"I'm ready to build the ramps. I have the plans; so if Evan will get the materials dropped off, I can get started," Travis said.

Rob made a note. "We'll see him at the prayer breakfast tomorrow, so you can tell him you're ready for the lumber, and I'll talk to the other guys about getting the painting done."

Molly nearly fell over. Rob and Evan were attending the men's prayer breakfast? Travis hadn't said anything to her about them joining the group.

"Yeah, he's getting to know some of the guys who've been volunteering with the house," Travis told her later.

"And you didn't think to tell me?"

"Don't make it into a big deal, Molls."

He was serious when he called her "Molls." It was his way of getting her attention. But what did he think she would do? Take out an ad in the Sunday paper? Travis was being ridiculous. Did Laney know about Rob and the prayer breakfast group?

"And, Molls, don't say anything to Laney. Rob will tell her what he wants when he wants." Well, of course, she wouldn't.

It was still exciting. Later, in the stillness of her dark bedroom, Molly lay thinking about what a wonderful day this had turned out to be. Even with Ellie and her moody behavior and Travis' misunderstanding. Things were improving. Laney would be coming home in a couple of weeks. Rob was going to the Tuesday morning men's breakfast. Everything would be okay after all.

Ringing interrupted Molly's sleep. Was she dreaming?

Molly reached for the phone. "Hello?" She struggled to raise herself up in the bed and see the clock. 3:00 a.m. Travis stirred beside her.

The words had her fully awake in seconds.

This was no dream.

It was a nightmare.

Chapter 15

ROB AND TRAVIS RUSHED TO the emergency room. Molly sat next to the phone. When it rang, she jumped.

"Travis? What happened?"

"They are not sure. She pulled herself out of bed and fell. She hit her head, so they are doing a CAT scan. I'll call you when I know something."

Sleep was out of the question. Molly turned on the television. Nothing.

She tackled her spice cabinet. She unloaded everything, read the expiration dates on each container, threw away two old cough drops she found near the back, and wiped the shelves clean.

An hour passed before Travis called back. "Her head's okay, but she's delirious."

"What do you mean?"

"She keeps saying things like there's a goat under her bed. Rob's with her now. I came out to call you. They're doing more tests."

"A reaction to medicine or something?"

"Maybe. You get some sleep. We're staying here. I'll call you soon."

Molly tried to sleep. She turned over. She punched her pillow. She eyed the clock. In two hours, Hunter and Ellie would be up and ready for school. She closed her eyes. Images of Laney lying in the emergency room being poked and prodded prohibited anything close to rest.

Molly caught up with Rob in the waiting room once she dropped the kids off at school.

"Laney has a UTI," Rob said.

"A urinary tract infection? What about her head injury?"

"Her head's fine. She has a bump, but it's the infection causing her to talk crazy." Rob shoved his head in his hands.

Molly shook her head. "Where's Travis?"

"He went home to get a shower before the prayer breakfast."

"Well, I'm here now. If you want to go, I'll stay here." Travis' warning sounded in her head. "I mean, if you need to grab a nap or something."

"I'm not going anywhere." Rob stood. "Sorry the call woke you. Guess I left my cell in the car."

Rob and Molly took turns, quietly watching as Laney slept the day away.

Travis called from work. "Now that they know what it is, she'll be okay. I'll tell Lissa." His confidence gave Molly hope.

That afternoon, Beverly came rolling into the room. Laney opened her eyes briefly.

"What you doin' laying in that bed, girl? Don't you be thinking 'bout taking a few days off here!"

Laney offered a weak smile, then closed her eyes and fell again into a deep sleep. Beverly signaled Rob and Molly outside.

"This here UTI is real common with paraplegics. We don't feel the symptoms the way you might. We jus' hafta watch carefully. Those antibiotics they givin' her are stronger than what you get at the drugstore, so they gonna keep her doped up today. But you watch. Tomorrow, she gonna be feeling better."

"Will they send her back to rehab then?" Rob asked.

"Prob'ly not for a few days. Remember, she's got no spleen. Infection like this is hard on that little body of hers. They'll keep her here a while until that ol' infection is cleared up. She'll be too weak, anyway."

"So this *will* set her back." Molly sighed. "She's worked so hard."

Beverly chuckled. "Miss Laney is one determined woman. She'll be fine. All she wants to do is get home to her family." Looking to Rob, she added, "She loves you and those babies more than life itself."

Rob pulled his mouth tight and stared down the empty corridor.

Laney perked up as Beverly predicted. The nurse on duty in the mornings was all business. The nurse on the evening shift, Joanie, was the exact opposite—warm and engaging. She made Laney feel as though she was the hospital's favorite patient—bringing her popsicles, fluffing her pillows, and massaging her neck.

"I don't want to burst your bubble," Molly said, "but I bet Joanie treats all her patients great."

"Yeah, I look forward to 'the sergeant' leaving every day and Joanie coming in. This morning, Ol' Sarge really got to me. She said she knew someone like me whose husband left her when he realized how hard it was to take care of her."

Molly wanted to punch the nurse in the nose. "She obviously doesn't know Rob."

"Actually, I think she was trying to say I'm lucky to have a guy like Rob, but the way it came out . . . It sounded more like, 'enjoy it while you can because this won't last.'"

"Oh, honey." Molly lightly touched Laney's arm.

"Beverly came in, and I told her. She rolled her eyes and said, 'I know the one you're talking about. I can take her!' then started moving toward the door."

"I can hear her now." Both women chuckled at the thought.

"This UTI has messed me up, though. I'm still weak and tired from it." Laney laid her head back on the pillow. "I'll never get out of here." Laney gripped the sheet in her fist and squeezed her eyes shut. "I'll never go home again."

Molly laid her hand over Laney's, and her daughter grabbed it and held tightly. Molly swallowed hard, searching for words of assurance. "You'll go home soon, Laney. Rob and your dad and Evan and a whole lot of people are working hard to get your house ready for you. You'll see. You'll go home." Molly stroked Laney's hair.

Eventually, Laney relaxed. She blew her nose and asked for a washcloth for her face. Molly sat by her side until she finally drifted to sleep.

Molly's heart ached, heavy with the negative thought "Ol' Sarge" had planted. Rob seemed dedicated—committed to Laney—but *would* it all grow old? He *was* young and active. Would he decide he had better things to do than to care for Laney one day?

Rainy days kept Travis from getting started on the ramp. Instead, he helped hang the kitchen cabinets and stain the woodwork for the new bathroom area.

"I have to keep busy, or I'm afraid I'll go crazy." Travis watched Molly clean the carrots. "I feel helpless at the hospital. When I'm working on the house, I'm doing something productive."

"I'm sure she understands."

Travis frowned. "I just can't sit there like you do."

"Nobody's asking you to, Travis. I think it's great the way Evan is letting you do so much. It's comforting to Laney to know you're there. You know how much she loves that house."

Travis snagged a carrot before Molly dumped them into the steamer. "Evan reminded me every nail is one step closer to bringing Laney home."

Molly stopped by to check on the ramp project the next afternoon—the first dry day in April. She sat on the step and watched as Travis shoved the posthole digger into the soft earth. "The doctor will probably release Laney tomorrow."

Travis looked up. "Release her?"

"From the hospital. She'll go back to the rehab unit."

"Think she'll still be home before Easter?"

"I doubt it." Molly reached down to pull an errant weed. "Maybe I should work on this flowerbed."

"Maybe you should come help me measure the depth of this hole."

The two worked until twilight digging the holes, pouring the concrete and setting the posts in place. Tammy brought Hunter and Ellie over to the house around seven o'clock.

"We had pizza for dinner, and then I took the kids to the park."

Molly looked at her grandchildren. They should change their names to "pizza" and "mac n' cheese." Ellie's pink T-shirt was highlighted with red pizza sauce, and her hair hung limp around her face.

"I have to go to Boston next week, but I told the kids I'll take them swimming at the Y tomorrow if it's okay with you," Tammy continued. She had picked the children up every day since Laney's emergency room crisis.

"That's a great idea. Would you two like that?" Molly asked.

"I want to see Mommy," Ellie whined. "Aunt Tammy wouldn't take us."

"Your mommy has been sick." Molly got down at eye level with her granddaughter. "Remember how we told you she has an infection?"

"We could wear the mask and gloves and stuff."

"It won't be much longer, sweetie. I promise." Molly hoped it was a promise she could keep.

She studied the kids' faces. They hadn't complained about being shifted from one house to another or never knowing who was picking them up and when. But Hunter's grades were slipping, and Ellie's teacher wanted a conference.

"Can we go inside and see our rooms?" Hunter asked.

"Sure. Go ahead." The kids said goodbye to Tammy and sprinted toward the front door. *See their rooms?*

"I'm worried about the kids," Molly told Travis as Tammy pulled out of the drive. "Hunter talked back to Tammy today. He never does that. And Ellie's teacher sent a note home."

"I wouldn't worry. Kids manage."

Molly wasn't so sure. Kids may "manage" when a goldfish dies or they lose a soccer game, but Hunter and Ellie had been virtually separated from their mother for over two months.

The children lived at their grandparents' house full-time; their mother now battled a dangerous infection; and Travis and Rob spent more and more and more time away from them, getting the house ready.

"Maybe next week, we can get them back into a routine. It's been great having Tammy help out, but . . . "

"And Laney may be back in rehab. That should help."

Would getting back to a routine be enough? She loaded the children into the car with their backpacks and swimsuits for the Y the next day. The remainder of the evening would be consumed with homework and baths at her house.

Rob stayed at the hospital. Since Molly would be putting the children to bed, she decided to add a prayer to their bedtime routine. She'd done it before.

But she should arm herself. The children might refuse.

At her request, Hunter joined her in Ellie's room. "You know how we pray at church? And how Grandpa prays at dinner?" she began. "Well, I thought it would be nice if we would say a little prayer before we go to bed."

"Mommy used to say nighttime prayers with us, but now Dad does," Hunter told her.

"When Daddy prays with us, we always pray for Mommy," Ellie added.

She had thought Laney so far from God she wouldn't teach prayers to her children. And Rob? She obviously didn't know her daughter and son-in-law as well as she thought. She had been prepared to teach them the little rhyming prayer she had said to her own girls when they were young.

Hunter folded his hands and started praying. "Thank You, God, for Mommy and Daddy and for Daddy and Grandpa working on the house to make it good for Mommy."

"And make Mommy well," Ellie added. "And thank You for Aunt Liss and Aunt Tammy."

So much for needing the rhyme.

"And, God, please make Grams happy again," Hunter said. "Amen."

"Amen!" Ellie jumped in her bed as Hunter hugged Molly and headed to his own room.

Later, she told Travis what Hunter prayed. "Do I seem unhappy?"

"No. They're not used to you being the one to tell them to eat their vegetables."

"Maybe that's it. Maybe I've been more mother than grandmother lately."

She hoped that's all it was.

With Rob still at the hospital, Molly took the children to school the next morning. She stopped by the school office to set up the conferences. The receptionist handed Molly a paper with one date and two times on it. "I figured you would prefer to meet both teachers on the same day."

Molly looked at the schedule. Maybe Travis could take the kids somewhere after school, so she could talk freely.

"How is Mrs. Camden?"

Molly smiled. "She's coming home soon."

"How wonderful! I've been praying for her."

"Thank you. She needs all the prayers she can get." Molly tucked the folded paper in her purse and left.

So many people were praying for Laney. She thought of Hunter and Ellie's prayer last night. So tender. So heartfelt. Ever since the onset of the infection, Molly's own prayers had been back to quick pleas for help. She had set aside her Bible reading in favor of working more on the house or sitting by Laney's side in the hospital.

She had turned into one of those 911 Christians she so often criticized. A modern-day Israelite wandering aimlessly in her own personal desert.

Chapter 16

ROB TEXTED FRIDAY AFTERNOON TO say that although Laney had returned to the rehab unit, she was in a different room. Molly stopped by after work, but Laney was asleep in the bed and Rob in the chair.

She tiptoed back into the hall and made a new plan. Since Tammy was taking the children to the Y, Molly drove home, changed into her "grubbies," loaded her gardening supplies into the trunk, and headed to the house to meet up with her husband.

The unfinished ramp was taking shape. When Molly pulled into the driveway, Travis was fighting with his circular saw.

"Wow! This looks good."

He didn't acknowledge her—just kept struggling with the tool in his hand, a scowl on his face.

"What's wrong, Travis?"

"This stupid blade! This is the second time it broke, and now I can't get the new one in!"

Molly was at a loss as to how to help. She started back to the car to unload her own yard tools.

"Nothing is going right!" Travis yelled. "Nothing!" He sounded desperate. Frustrated.

Molly wheeled around, afraid he would cut himself with the saw in his anger. "It looks great."

Travis slammed the saw down and sat on the step, covering his face with his hands. "The saw isn't working." He waved his hand over the decking. "I cut those pieces on the end wrong and had to do that whole section over. Nothing's right."

"Maybe you just need a break." Molly rubbed the back of his neck.

"Maybe I shouldn't be doing this at all." Travis lifted his head up, and his lip trembled. Molly sat and put her arms around him.

"It will be okay, Travis." Her voice was soft and even. "Maybe you should just go buy a new saw."

"I can't fix it. I can't fix anything. My little girl's lying there in that bed apologizing to me, saying she let me down, and here I am making a mess of one little job."

A tear escaped. Molly's chest tightened. She could count on one hand the times she had seen Travis cry.

"I'm sorry. It's just seeing her there and knowing she'll never walk again. I talk a good game, Molls, but . . . " He slammed a fist onto the porch. "Sometimes, I just want to shout at God. I mean, where was He?"

How could she help him when she couldn't help herself? "Maybe we should get a fresh start in the morning."

"No. I'm doing this. I can't do anything else for Laney. I can do this." Travis stood, turned away, and wiped his face with the sleeve of his shirt. He picked up the saw once more and worked at attaching the new blade. What could she do? Travis had a collection of CDs in his car. Maybe some music would soothe him. She went into the house to look for a player.

Molly gasped. The entire area had been totally cleared of building debris. She could see through to the new granite countertops in the kitchen.

Molly walked through the space and inspected the newly renovated bathroom, touching the vanity designed so Laney could easily reach everything from her wheelchair. She flipped the lowered light switch in the bedroom and walked across the hardwood floors into the freshly painted space. The closet doors were still in boxes leaning against the interior of the closet.

Upstairs, everything looked the same. She found a CD player in Hunter's room, an extension cord in the kitchen. She stretched the cord as far as she could, which brought it out the front door to the edge of the existing porch. Soon, the sounds of a smooth jazz CD floated over the front yard. It was all she could do.

Travis pushed on with his work.

Molly donned her garden gloves and began digging in the flowerbed next to the steps.

"The house is really starting to look great, isn't it?"

Travis didn't answer. The humming of his saw stopped. Molly followed his gaze and noticed a small, white car driving slowly past the house. The woman driving looked strangely familiar.

"That's about the fourth time today she's driven by here and slowed down," Travis said. "Wonder what she wants."

"Probably just a curious neighbor," Molly suggested. "She looks familiar, but I can't place her. Maybe I met her when they had that neighborhood yard sale."

"Well, she keeps giving me the evil eye."

"She's probably worried about what you're doing to this old house. You know, one of the reservationist types."

"Did you say 'reservationist types'?" Travis laughed. "You mean preservationist, don't you?"

"I think we're both tired." Molly attacked the dirt once again with the corner of the spade, happy to hear her husband's laughter. Her tension dissipated alongside his.

With the children safely in Rob and Tammy's care, Travis and Molly worked until darkness overtook them. They packed up their tools and headed home, where they pulled leftover meatloaf from the refrigerator and made sandwiches.

Travis brought two bottles of cold water to the table. "Hard work makes for a good kind of tired."

"Speak for yourself. I'm just glad tomorrow is Saturday, so I can sleep in!"

Travis played the messages on the answering machine as they ate together. The first two were hang-ups. "We have gotten several of those lately."

The next message was from Lissa's friend. "Hello there. This is Mark Meiers. I'm going to be in the Cincinnati area next week, and I was hoping we could get together. I'd like to take the two of you out for dinner. I'll try to call again tomorrow."

Molly put her hand over her mouth. "Oh, my!"

"What's wrong with that?"

"He's going to ask permission to marry Lissa," Molly whispered.

"What makes you think that, and why are you whispering?"

"I don't know. I just have a feeling that's why he's coming."

"Look, he could be coming here for anything. He could be meeting with someone at the university, or it could have something to do with his research, or, well, anything."

Molly bit into her sandwich. There was an outside chance Travis was right, but her intuition told her to start thinking about wedding plans for her younger daughter.

"Just in case, though," Travis said with a grin, "maybe you shouldn't say anything to anyone about his coming. Especially Lissa."

Molly awoke Saturday morning to silence. A note on the table from Travis confirmed his plans to finish the ramp this morning. Rob had taken the kids out for breakfast at Bob's Pancake House, then to see their mother for a couple of hours. Molly decided to visit Laney in the afternoon.

Molly ate a banana and a bowl of cereal and looked around. How long had it been since she had given the kitchen a deep cleaning? Or any other part of the house, for that matter? There was no putting it off.

She changed the sheets and ran the vacuum under the bed Hunter used. The hose clogged. A quick investigation found a wad of paper stuck in the beater bar attachment. She looked under the bed. Hunter's homework. A few math papers were in the pile, but most were lined notebook paper. All were blank except for Hunter's name scrawled in the upper righthand corner and the heading, "My mom is the greatest because . . ."

All morning, Molly turned over possible reasons Hunter hadn't finished the essay. Had he heard them talking about the accident? Maybe he was more frightened by his mother's paralysis than they knew. Worse yet, had someone at school said something about drunk driving?

Molly welcomed the work. If left to only think about the What Ifs, she would make herself sick.

Three hours later, when Rob called to say he and the children were headed to their own house, Molly looked with satisfaction at all she had accomplished in such a short time. Three loads of laundry were folded and put away; the bathrooms had been scrubbed; floors had been vacuumed; and furniture had been dusted.

Molly was in the middle of pulling everything out of the refrigerator when the phone rang again. Her hands were full of something slimy that may have once been a cucumber. She tossed the decomposed vegetable in the sink. She turned up her nose, wiped her hands with a paper towel, and grabbed the phone just before the recorder picked it up.

"Hello?" Molly spoke into the receiver, trying not to sound rushed or harried. No one answered. "Hello? Anybody there?"

Molly could hear someone breathing.

"Who is this?"

There was a loud click as the caller hung up abruptly. A shiver ran up Molly's spine. Molly thought perhaps the hang-ups on the machine had been computer calls for some sales company, but this call was different.

Clearly, someone was on the other end. A wave of uneasiness rolled over her. She was about to call Travis when the phone rang once more.

Chapter 17

"SO, WHAT DID LISSA HAVE to say?" Laney glanced out the window.

"Just checking in." She wouldn't mention Mark's impending visit. "So, how do you like your new digs?" she asked, looking around the room.

"Oh, you know, you've seen one of these rooms, you've seen them all. I'm so sick of being here."

Molly studied Laney's face, the dark shadows under her eyes. "Don't let it get to you, sweetheart. It won't be long before you are home."

"You keep saying that, Mom, but what if I go home and something like what happened last week happens again?"

"We'll deal with it. Have you seen Beverly?"

"Only *all* the time! I can't decide if she's diligent or pushy."

As if on cue, the energetic woman rolled into Laney's room.

"I was jus' passin' through. I come over to meet up with a boy over in the hospital. He was playin' up in the rafters of one of those old barns and came fallin' down three stories to the floor. Jus' lucky he didn't land on a pitchfork or somethin'. He'll be over here next week."

Laney frowned. "How old is he?"

"Ten. Isn't that close to your boy?"

"Is he paralyzed?"

"Paraplegic, jus' like you and me, 'cept he can't feel anything from the chest down. He got his arms though."

"Poor little guy," Molly whispered.

"Anyway, I come to get you to help me," Beverly told Laney.

"Me? I can't help!"

"You got a boy, don't you? I got only little girls."

"But what can I do?" Laney inquired.

"Jus' be yourself. His name is Eli." Beverly headed for the door. "I'll see you Monday."

"What could I possibly do to help?" Laney asked, turning to her mother.

"Talk to him? I don't know. What did Beverly do to get you through all of this?"

"Beverly says she doesn't do anything. She says it's God doin' all the doin', and she's just here to help."

"Well, maybe she's just asking you to help God here."

Laney rolled her eyes. "I have hydrotherapy in twenty minutes. It'll take me that long to get ready." Molly got the message. She pulled her sweater on, kissed Laney on the cheek, and headed for the door.

A ten-year-old boy. A little older than Hunter. Paralyzed. Laney had always been eager to help others. What made her hesitate now?

Molly went to bed early on Saturday. Tired from the heavy gardening and the housework, she was sure sleep would come the minute her head hit the pillow.

It didn't. Her mind raced. She made multiple lists in her head and tried to think through the schedule for the week ahead. She tossed and turned. First, she was hot; then her nightgown seemed to knot up under her.

She got up and went to the bathroom.

She tried once more to sleep.

Her thoughts turned to Lissa. Was Mark coming to Cincinnati next Wednesday for work or school? Or was he planning to ask Travis for Lissa's hand in marriage? Would Lissa want a big wedding? Laney's wedding had been so beautiful. Lissa had been her sister's maid of honor. Laney would be—Laney would be in a wheelchair. She flipped her pillow over to the cool side and kicked free of the sheets, resting her feet on top of them. The comforter lay in a pile against Travis' back.

She was no closer to sleep than when she had gone to bed the night before. Unfortunately, these kinds of sleepless nights were not foreign to Molly. At her last check-up, the doctor had talked about the symptoms of menopause. *Maybe I should have opted for the hormone therapy.*

The clock radio signaled morning. Molly followed Travis out of bed, but quickly returned. Her head pounded. Light shining from the bathroom made the sharp pain feel like a sword being thrust into her temple.

"I'm not sure I should leave you like this."

"Please go, Travis," she mumbled without lifting her head. "You don't need to miss church. You, Rob, and the kids go on. Just turn out the light, and let me sleep."

Before Christmas, when Molly had a similar headache, her doctor had given her samples of a migraine medicine and a prescription in case the debilitating pain continued. Happily, it hadn't.

She reached in the drawer of her nightstand and fished out one of the small foil packages. She struggled to separate the cardboard and foil. There were two tablets inside.

Molly's stomach churned as she made her way to the bathroom. Definitely a migraine.

Her glass was missing. *Argh, I cleaned yesterday.* The small glass she kept in the bathroom was now in the dishwasher. Molly cupped her hands beneath the water flowing from the spigot, washed down the pills, and made her way back to bed. Her head still screamed in pain after fifteen minutes had passed. She wet a washcloth with cold water, put it on her forehead, and fell back onto the mattress.

She was missing church. *Was this Palm Sunday? No, that's next week.*

Her head hurt. Her eyes hurt. She closed her eyes. *Please, God, make this go away.*

Hours later, Molly pulled herself up, and she sat on the edge of her bed. Someone was making noise in the kitchen. Molly wrapped her robe around herself and gingerly made her way down the stairs.

"There she is!" Travis called out as his wife rounded the corner of the kitchen. "How are you feeling?"

Molly cringed at Travis' loud voice. "Lazy."

"I'm making beanies and weenies for dinner. Are you hungry?"

"Not really." She wasn't sure she could stomach baked beans and hot dogs right now. "Where is everybody?"

"Rob's with Laney, and the kids are in the family room watching a movie."

Molly poked her head in the family room to check on her grand-children. "Well, if it's okay, I think I need to go back to bed."

Travis stopped stirring. "You look tired. Maybe you do need more sleep. Are you sure you don't want something to eat?"

"I'm sure. I'm sorry, Travis."

"Sorry for what?"

"Sorry for being sick and leaving you with everything."

"Hey, we're fine. Go back to bed."

She headed back to the bedroom. The top of her head felt cold. She located a brown wool cap for her cold head and snuggled under the comforter to rest for a few minutes.

The morning sun and the smell of coffee brewing aroused her from a deep, healing sleep. It took a few minutes for her eyes to focus on the clock radio.

Seven-thirty.

"Seven-thirty!" she cried out. She intended to be at work this morning by eight-thirty. Although she didn't punch a time clock, Molly had been compulsive about giving her company a full forty hours a week. She had used sick leave and a few vacation days since Laney's accident but worked hard to maintain continuity in the projects on her desk.

Molly raced to get ready, mentally reviewing her workload for the day. She had no meetings. That was a plus. She needed to set up a focus group for a company marketing disposable contact lenses, but had outlined a plan. She breathed a bit easier as she reviewed her day. She could still make it to the office by eight-thirty, but it would mean foregoing her morning visit with Laney.

Travis was already dressed and ready for the office when Molly came into the kitchen. He was reading the paper, his hand wrapped around his favorite mug.

"I thought you left."

"I have a meeting downtown with the city planner at ten." Travis kissed her. "I wanted to make sure you were okay before I took off. How's your headache?"

"Gone. I can't believe I slept so long. Did Rob leave with the kids?"

"A few minutes ago. You were in the shower."

Molly put a bagel in the toaster and sat down at the kitchen table with her coffee. "I feel so stupid."

"Why?"

"I lost a whole day. I can't believe I slept that long."

"Hey, you needed it. And don't worry. We can take care of ourselves."

Travis gave her a quick peck on the cheek and headed to work. Molly was close on his heels. She poured a second steaming cup of coffee in a travel mug and wrapped her hot bagel in a napkin to eat on the way. She called Laney to say she would not be by for breakfast. The week was off to a sketchy start.

"Hunter is distracted," Hunter's teacher told Molly the next afternoon. "I know he's been under a lot of stress with his mother in the hospital and all."

Molly looked around the cluttered room. She was mildly distracted herself. "I understand." She turned back to Mrs. O'Brien. "I thought if you could tell me what to do to help . . . " Her voice trailed as she looked to the gray-haired woman for answers.

Mrs. O'Brien pulled up her grade sheet on the computer. "Hunter is doing okay. He's struggling a bit in math. We are learning multiplication right now."

"We can help him learn his multiplication tables."

"We don't teach children to memorize those tables anymore, Mrs. Tipton. We're focusing on helping children understand the concept first."

"Well, I'm sure my husband can help him." Molly pulled out a wrinkled writing paper. "I was more worried about this."

"Oh, the writing project. Hunter's essay is fine. This must be an old draft. Don't tell Mrs. Camden, though. We are putting them all together in a book for Mother's Day."

Satisfied, Molly headed to Ellie's classroom.

Mrs. Caulfield shook Molly's hand. Molly sat down in a tiny red chair. Mrs. Caulfield sat in a little blue chair opposite her.

"I'm worried about Ellie," she began. "She is a good student, but she's becoming somewhat bossy. I noticed that she hardly plays with anyone on the playground, just walks around by herself."

"I'm sure this has to do with her mother being in the hospital." Molly's mind flew back to the fights Ellie had with Alex. "But she's back in the rehab unit, so we should be getting back into a routine now."

"Ellie told me her mother is never coming home."

Molly's mouth fell open. "What?"

"She said her mother has to live at the hospital; and someday, she's going to have Ellie come over for dinner."

Molly tried to see the events of the last few weeks from Ellie's perspective. To a five-year-old, a week probably seemed like a month. Two months? Like forever. "Actually, we're hoping Laney will be home in a couple of weeks."

"Sometimes, children act out when they feel they have no control over anything. I have an idea." Mrs. Caulfield had Molly's full attention. "Ellie is obsessed with our class hamster. What if . . . "

Please don't let her offer to give Ellie the creature as a gift to take home.

"What if I appointed Ellie the hamster's caretaker? Maybe if she could be in charge of him, she wouldn't feel the need to control everyone else."

"Couldn't that backfire? What if she thinks being bossy is what got her this new position?" Maybe the young educator hadn't thought this through.

"Ellie's a reasonable person. I think I can explain it to her and help her put words to her emotions."

A steady rain was coming down as Molly left the school parking lot. Mrs. Caulfield had called Ellie a reasonable person. Images of constant battles at the dinner table flashed through her mind.

Ellie? Reasonable? Molly couldn't see it.

Maybe the teacher was right. Maybe Ellie felt out of control. Isn't that how she felt? How do you teach a five-year-old not to expect to control everything? Or a fifty-nine-year-old grandmother?

Maybe that was something they could learn together.

Chapter 18

"LISSA TOLD ME THAT'S YOUR favorite. I've never tried it," Mark said as they waited for their table at the restaurant just north of Cincinnati. Well, that was as good as a confession of his true intentions for this meeting.

"How did you find this place?" Travis asked.

"The internet. I hope it's as good as it sounds."

"It certainly looks beautiful, and it's busy for a Wednesday evening." Molly reached out to touch the leaf of a bamboo shoot. The host arrived to escort them to their table. Strains of oriental music offered a soft background to quiet conversations around them.

Travis asked Mark about his work, leading the men into a discussion about a complicated engineering question. Molly looked over the menu. She effectively tuned out the engineering talk until she heard Mark say something about "meeting with a colleague in Columbus."

"I contacted a researcher at Ohio State about a project."

"So, you're staying in Columbus?" Molly asked.

"Just tonight. I drove straight here from Morgantown. I'll drive back tomorrow afternoon."

The waiter filled the water glasses. Maybe she had been wrong about Mark's visit. Perhaps he was, as Travis said, just in town and wanted to get together. Still, he had driven two extra hours out of his way to meet them at a restaurant serving their favorite food.

All three studied the menu.

"So, how spicy is spicy, Travis?" Mark asked. "Someone said something about ordering by the numbers?"

"One isn't hot at all, and I think the numbers go up to ten. Molly used to ask for a zero, but she's worked her way up to a two."

Molly acted deeply offended. "I like to taste my food."

"True." Travis placed his napkin in his lap. "I've seen guys I work with order a ten, and they break out in a sweat just trying to have lunch."

"So, what number do you get?" Mark asked.

"Me? I'm a five."

"Maybe for my first time eating Thai food, I'll go with a three. What do you think?"

That he was a man not easily sucked into macho games. He was his own person, and she liked that.

When the server returned, all three ordered the Chicken Pad Thai. While they waited for the food to arrive, they talked about Lissa and her research project, how Laney was progressing, and basketball. Usually, Rob and Travis closely followed the Cincinnati Bearcats during March Madness; but this year, the only team they had followed was Hunter's.

They were still on the subject of basketball when their colorful plates of food arrived. Mark tasted the chicken.

"Well?" asked Molly.

"Very good. It's sweeter than I expected."

Travis wasn't going to pass up the opportunity to talk Bearcat basketball, so the conversation returned to the college coaches who had left or been fired and the likelihood of a Bearcat comeback next season.

"I would have figured you for a WVU fan," Travis said.

"Oh, I've watched the Mountaineers play; but I grew up in Indiana, so I'm really a Hoosier at heart. Lissa's a big Bearcats fan, so they've sort of become a team I follow." *He follows the Bearcats because Lissa is a fan. More proof.*

Once they had finished their main course, the server convinced them to try the sticky rice. They ordered tea to accompany the sweet dessert.

Mark took a sip of tea as the server placed the sticky rice in front of them. He took a bite of the dessert, took another sip of tea, and fidgeted with his napkin. "Well, I think you know how I feel about your daughter," Mark began.

Travis offered a slow nod of the head, but Molly simply took the tiny fork and began to dig into her dessert. She looked at the scoop of sticky rice on the plate, not at Mark, for fear she would cry or laugh or blurt out, "I knew it!" She poked at the rice and smiled.

"Wow, this is harder than I expected." Mark ate another bite of the rice. He put his fork down and sipped his tea. Molly and Travis remained silent. "I love Melissa. I love her, and I want to ask your permission to marry her. I know I can be a good husband to her. I want to make her happy. But I want your blessing. I won't ask her unless I have your blessing." Mark's words tumbled out in a torrent. He had probably rehearsed what he wanted to say his entire five hours of driving time.

Molly looked to Travis. Then they both turned their eyes to Mark and smiled. It should have been a solemn moment, but Molly struggled to stifle a giggle.

"You have our blessing," Travis told their future son-in-law. He handed Mark a napkin. "Here, you might want to get the sticky rice out of your beard."

Mark wiped his face. "That's embarrassing!"

"No, Mark, that's just family!" Molly patted his hand. "We couldn't have picked a better man for Lissa."

Mark took another a sip of tea. He relaxed his shoulders. "Actually, I feel like God brought us together. She is the most incredible woman I have ever known."

"Will you live in West Virginia?" Travis squeezed Molly's hand.

"I haven't asked her to marry me yet. But I know she would like to live here. Near Laney. She says Laney will need her. I may look around the area to see what I can find in my field. UC has already expressed an interest in me teaching there."

"The University of Cincinnati? That would be great! Be sure to tell them you're already a Bearcat fan," Travis advised.

On leaving, Travis and Molly promised they wouldn't tell anyone about Mark's intentions. It would be a hard secret to keep.

Travis opened the car door for Molly. "Well, you were right."

He and Molly relived the conversation of the evening as they drove home. Travis turned the car's heater on low. "They'll probably wait until Lissa finishes her thesis and gets a job."

Molly gazed out the window. "Maybe. But I'm guessing the wedding will take place within the year."

The renovations were nearly complete. Evan's crew had cleared out. All that was left was finishing the ramp entry to the kitchen's back entrance and moving the bedroom furniture. Rob looked into the cost of a stairway chair lift. If the device could be installed in their house, the second floor wouldn't be off limits to Laney.

Laney held the pictures her mother had taken once the construction crew had left. "Oh, Mom, it looks even more spacious than I imagined!"

"I almost didn't show you these. I thought about trying to surprise you like one of those home decorating shows on TV."

"I don't think I'm ready to be part of a reality show," Laney said.

The men moved the bedroom furniture into the new master suite that evening. Rob ordered a new mattress and box springs to meet Laney's needs. It would arrive by the end of the week. Molly purchased new sheets and a colorful coverlet as Laney's welcome home gift.

Molly took the children with her after school on Friday to clean their bedrooms. While they worked at putting all of their toys and books away, Molly moved Rob and Laney's clothes from the upstairs closet to the new bedroom. She left the assortment of bridesmaid's dresses and maternity clothes Laney had shoved in the back of the small space. The new closet was spacious and featured a motorized bar, much like a rotisserie in an oven. *Evan had vision.*

Molly turned her attention to the floor of the upstairs clothes closet. Only the shoes were left. Molly sat down and picked up a pair of Laney's high-heeled shoes and hugged them to her chest. Her eyes burned with unshed tears. She chewed her lower lip. A picture of Laney clomping around in Molly's high heels as a toddler came unbidden to her mind. The blue heels she and Laney had dyed to match her prom dress tugged at her memory. The white satin heels Laney chose for her wedding.

Shoes tell the story of our lives.

Ellie came running into the now-empty bedroom, screaming, "Hunter hit me!" He was fast behind her. "She hit me first!"

Molly closed her eyes tight.

"No hitting. I don't even want to know what happened. Just no hitting." She pushed herself up from the bedroom floor. Both children started talking at the same time.

Molly spun. "Stop it!" She bent down to within inches of their startled faces and spoke through clenched teeth, her voice even and firm. "I *do not* want to know what happened. I only want you to stop yelling at each other and remember this one rule: No hitting." She turned and headed down the stairs, leaving a startled Hunter and Ellie standing in the middle of the empty room.

Downstairs, Molly went into the bathroom and closed the door. She shook. Never before had she been that close to losing her temper with Hunter and Ellie. Would they hate her for it? Hands on the sink's edge, Molly leaned heavily on the new granite surface.

A pang of self-pity knifed her heart. Hadn't she already raised her own children? Slowly raising her head, Molly studied her image in the mirror. What was it she had been thinking about before the children started fighting?

It was the shoes. Images of Laney's first steps in the high-top, stiff, white shoes of a toddler flashed before her. Laney's first ballet slippers. There were new school shoes each September, white patent leathers every year for Easter, and black patent leathers for Christmas.

Molly wiped her face.

It was the shoes triggering her anger, not the children. The shoes were a reminder of all Laney had been and had become. The shoes she would never wear again to a dance or to take a run in the park. The shoes were to blame.

Molly took a deep breath and left her hideaway.

She found the kids working diligently together to put fresh sheets on Ellie's bed.

"Look, Grams. Hunter's helping me push the wrinkles out."

"We're sorry, Grams."

"I know, Hunter. Look, I'm sorry, too. I was a little upset," Molly confessed. They threw their arms around her.

"That's okay. Sometimes, Hunter gets a little upset, too," Ellie offered. Hunter gave his little sister a look, but Molly hugged them a bit harder and began to laugh.

"Let's just finish our jobs, and then I vote we pick up sandwiches on the way home."

Molly returned to the offensive shoes and selected two pairs of tennis shoes, two pair of flats, and a pair of slippers to move downstairs to the now accessible shoe rack Evan had installed. The rest she put in a blue laundry basket she found in the attic stairway. She moved Rob's shoes to his side of the closet in the new downstairs bedroom.

She wandered back into Rob and Laney's old room. When the men moved the furniture, they had moved items from the top of the dresser and chest and put them in piles on the floor.

She smiled as she picked up the picture frames with family photos. Two were of Hunter and Ellie, and one frame held the last family portrait they had taken when Ellie was a baby. A larger version of the one she had on her work desk.

Molly lifted a framed picture of Rob and Laney on their wedding day. She set the picture aside to take downstairs with the others later and looked at the stack of papers it had been covering. Curious, she picked up an unopened envelope on the top of the pile. The return address was Midville Medical Group. She looked through the pile of medical bills—some opened, some still sealed in their envelopes. Molly couldn't help but notice the charges on some of the pages. She knew Laney's health care would be expensive, but these bills represented thousands of dollars.

What was going on here? Why were these bills piled up like this, and why were so many of them unopened? She needed some answers.

Chapter 19

"WHY CAN'T I JOIN THE swim team?" Hunter threw the YMCA flyer at Molly.

"I said we'll wait and see."

"You're not my mom!" Hunter stomped off to the guest room he shared with his dad.

Molly gritted her teeth and stared at the crumpled paper in her hand. Practices started after spring break. This would have to be Rob's decision.

Rob didn't answer Hunter when the subject came up. Instead, he promised to take Hunter and Ellie to the open swim time at the YMCA on Saturday morning.

"I'll have to check out your strokes. See if you're ready."

With a little begging on Ellie's part, Travis agreed to accompany them. He was anxious to finish the back ramp at the house, but Molly convinced him an hour or two at the pool with the grandchildren would benefit everyone.

"While you're with Rob, you could give him a little fatherly advice." Molly picked up the crayons Ellie left strewn on the family room floor.

"Is this about the bills you found at their house?"

"Travis, the hospital costs alone are astronomical."

"Rob will handle it."

"Maybe. But he's never faced anything like this before. We have, with Mom. His parents are gone. He looks up to you like a father. At least think about it."

"I'll pray about it."

Pray about it? Molly wanted him to *do* something about it. Molly whispered a prayer of her own. "Help Travis talk to Rob," she begged.

Not that she expected an answer. God could be almost as stubborn as Travis.

Finding Saturday morning to herself, Molly put six chicken breasts in her slow cooker and headed out the door to enjoy a long, leisurely visit with Laney.

Approaching Laney's room, Molly heard someone praying. She peeked in. Sitting side-by-side in their wheelchairs, heads bowed, Laney and Beverly were holding hands. Each had an open Bible on her lap.

Molly let out a little gasp but quickly covered her mouth.

Had the unstoppable Beverly been able to engage Laney in Bible study? Was this a first, or was it a regular event? Maybe she needed a Beverly to jumpstart her own spiritual life.

She headed for the coffee shop in the main hospital to give the two women a little space. Molly treated herself to a Caramel Macchiato. The sweet caramel flavor of the coffee was worth the four-dollar price tag.

For a moment, Molly wanted to pretend she was in another place and time, not in a hospital coffee shop wasting time until she could visit her paralyzed child. Someone had left a newspaper behind. A section of advertisements fell out of the center of the paper when she picked it up.

A half hour later, Molly made her way back to Laney's room. She met Beverly midway down the hall.

"Hello there, girl! You won't find Miss Laney in her room. I got her workin'."

"Eli?"

"Yep. She's good for that boy! Talks to him 'bout all kinds of stuff. Turns out he's good in math, so she's gonna see if he'll help her boy with his multiplying."

"I'm glad she found a way to get the children together. She told me last night she was afraid the kids would be jealous of the time she's been spending with Eli." An angry Hunter stomping his way up the stairs came to mind. "Do you think she'll be long?"

"Nah. She was jus' trying to catch him before he went to therapy."

Saying her goodbyes, Molly waited in Laney's room. She looked through the ads she had kept from the paper. Forty minutes passed.

"Mom! How long have you been here?"

"Not long," Molly lied.

"I didn't know you were coming. Rob called on the way to the Y. This was your chance to sleep in for a change."

"I know, but I decided to spend a little time with you. When I stop by in the mornings, I have to rush to work. Today, I have nothing on my plate. How about you?"

Laney threw her hands up in the air. "I'm as free as a bird! What did you have in mind?"

"I brought these." Molly waved the ads in the air. "I thought we could plan Easter baskets. You pick out what you want, and I'll do the shopping."

Laney took the colorful advertisements her mother handed her. Her forehead wrinkled. "I thought I would be home by now. I wanted to shop for their Easter things."

"You will," Molly assured her. "This year, you'll shop via your personal shopper. And next year, you'll be on your own."

Laney inhaled and let out a slow, even breath. "Okay. Let's go down to the common room and make a list."

The large, rectangular room was furnished at one end with tables and upholstered chairs. The other end featured several groupings of chairs where visitors could spend time with the patients—or clients, as Beverly called them.

Laney maneuvered her wheelchair up to one of the unoccupied tables. Molly took a seat and spread the newspaper out on the table. She searched her purse for a piece of paper, but finding none, pulled out an old envelope instead.

They spent the next hour going through the ads, picking out the best buys.

"Remember the year it snowed on Easter Sunday, and you and Dad hid the eggs all over the house?"

"And remember the year your grandma brought those giant stuffed rabbits?"

"I remember," answered Laney wistfully. "I miss Grandma."

"Me, too."

Laney rescued them from the moment with another memory. "I remember the time Lissa got in a fight with Matt at church just before the Palm Sunday procession, and they went down the aisle bashing each other all the way with palm fronds."

"They were lucky Miss Jane had run out of the real ones, and they had silk ones. The real ones could have hurt!"

"What is really hilarious about that is that they wound up going to prom together." Laney was laughing so hard, she had to hold her stomach. "I always thought if they got married, I would use that bit in a toast at the reception."

Molly fought the urge to tell Laney about Mark's visit. "Are the kids going to be in the Palm Sunday procession this year?"

"I hope so. I told Rob to video it for me."

Molly reviewed her list. "What about Easter eggs? Should we get that plastic kind and fill them with candy?"

"A few, maybe, but I'm going to boil some eggs here for Hunter, Ellie, and Eli to color next week."

"How is Eli doing?"

"Actually, he's doing better than I did my first week. His mother is a mess, though. She blames herself for his accident."

"Why? I thought he fell off of a barn rafter."

"He did. But he had been pestering her to go somewhere, and she had things to do. She told him to go out and play and stop bugging her. When she went looking, she heard him calling for help from the barn. He was lying on the hard, wooden floor and could not move."

"How awful." Molly couldn't imagine the roller coaster of emotions Eli's mother had to be experiencing.

"The counselors are good here, but maybe you could talk to her, Mom."

"Me? I wouldn't know where to begin, Laney."

"Hmm, what was it you said to me only a few days ago? Something about helping God?"

For the Palm Sunday service, the choir sang three songs from the cantata they would perform on Easter Sunday. Pastor Haynes talked about the week Jesus entered Jerusalem. Members of the drama team were planted throughout the auditorium. On cue, a member of the team would stand and quote a Scripture concerning the Person of Christ.

"Don't you love this?" Travis whispered.

She glanced toward the back of the auditorium. Again. Finally, one of the actors stood and said, "Behold the Lamb of God!"

The doors at the back of the room opened, and the children paraded in, waving the palm fronds high above their heads, saying, "Hosanna! Hosanna in the highest!" Once they reached the front of the room, they climbed on the risers set up on the floor below the stage.

Molly searched the faces. Hunter stood in the middle row, stiff. The children sang the praise song they had learned in Sunday school. Hunter didn't open his mouth.

Ellie, in the front row, moved and swayed with the music, waving her palm frond so aggressively, the leader had to take it from her. As the children finished the song, a bearded, white-clad "Jesus" walked down the aisle and took a seat in the midst of the children. Ellie jumped up into his open arms, causing Jesus to lose his balance momentarily. A smiling Rob caught it all on video.

Hunter and Ellie's spring break coincided with the Easter holiday. Rob arranged to have the children stay with Ellie's sitter on Tuesday and Thursday. Rob's sister would have them on Friday. That left Monday and Wednesday for Travis and Molly to figure out a work and childcare schedule.

Monday morning, Molly took the kids to have breakfast with their mother. Carrying a bag of doughnuts and a thermos of orange juice, the three joined Laney as she ate her oatmeal.

After breakfast, Laney took them to the common area. She maneuvered her wheelchair down the corridor to Eli's room and disappeared inside for a few minutes.

When she returned, Eli followed close behind. The children had met briefly only once before. All three youngsters were quiet for a moment.

"Hi," Eli said shyly.

"I like your chair," said Ellie. "Can you roll fast like my mom?"

Eli smiled. "Faster." He looked at Laney with the hint of a challenge in his eyes.

"Don't even think about it." Laney left the kids to talk for a few minutes before putting her plan into action. She pulled Hunter aside and spoke to him in low tones, kissed him on the cheek, and thanked him.

"Hey, Eli," Hunter said, "My mom says you can help me with multiplication."

Eli held up the bag of jellybeans and a stack of little plastic medicine cups he had carried on his lap. "That's why I brought these." Eli moved over to the table where Hunter and Ellie joined him. Carefully, he counted out a pile of jellybeans. Laney provided a pad of paper and a pencil.

"Do I get some, too?" Ellie asked. Always watchful to make sure Hunter and his friends treated her fairly.

"In a minute," Eli said, but then handed her one of the sweet candies. She popped it in her mouth and waited to see what Eli would do next.

Eli put three of the little plastic cups in front of him. He began distributing the beans. "One, one, one. Two, two, two. Three, three, three. Four, four, four. Five, five, five. Now, how many beans are there?" Eli asked.

Ellie started to reach for the first cup to count each bean.

"How many beans are in each cup?" Eli asked Hunter.

Hunter leaned over the table and peered into the cups. "Five," he announced.

"If we want to figure out how many beans there are, we could dump them all out and count or we could just add five together three times. Do you know how to count by fives?"

"Sure. Five, ten, fifteen, twenty, twenty-five," Hunter began. He stopped, pointed to the cups and said, "Fifteen! I get it."

"Is that all there is to it?" Hunter stared at the cups of candies.

"Pretty much. If you have a multiplication problem, you're just adding one of the numbers together as many times as it says."

The three children began making up new problems for Hunter to solve. They had eaten their way through half the bag of jellybeans when Eli's therapist came for him.

"Hey, Eli. Maybe sometime you can come over to my house to play," Hunter said as Eli rolled away.

"That went well," Molly said as the children began cleaning up the table.

"He's a neat kid," Laney replied. "I'm glad Hunter likes him. They could be good for each other."

Chapter 20

MOLLY PURCHASED BASKETS, GRASS, CANDY, plastic eggs, a few small toys, an egg coloring kit, and two dozen eggs. Although it wasn't on the official Easter basket list, Molly found an activity book on multiplication for Hunter and a coloring alphabet book for Ellie. She was all the way out to the car when she decided to go back and purchase three chocolate Easter bunnies: one for Hunter, one for Ellie, and one for Eli.

Okay, four chocolate bunnies. One for Travis.

Rob called to say Laney was cooking for them in the family life center. "Meatloaf again. You and Travis can come, too."

"I think we'll take a rain check. Travis is trying to finish the back ramp."

The April air was warm. She called Travis to tell him she would meet him at Laney's house, then packed her picnic basket with cold leftover fried chicken and baked beans. She threw in a couple of apples and filled a thermos with freshly brewed coffee. Within the hour, Travis and Molly were sitting on the back deck enjoying the quiet evening and the makeshift picnic.

"Travis, I saw that woman in the white car again. She was parked across the street when I got here but drove off when I pulled in the drive. She gives me the creeps."

"Me, too, but you were probably right the first time. Just a nosey neighbor." Travis stretched. "I'm so tired, Molly."

"You should be. You've been working hard."

"It's not the work. It's the waiting. The accident was only a few months ago, but it feels like years have passed."

On Wednesday morning, the hospital number on Molly's office caller ID brought with it a moment of panic. She grabbed the receiver.

"This is Molly Tipton."

"Mom! I had to call you." Laney's voice was breathless on the other end.

"Are you okay? I saw the hospital number and—"

"Sorry. I couldn't wait. I'm calling from the therapy room. I just had my evaluation, and I get to go home!"

"When?" Molly asked, dropping her papers on the desk.

"Maybe as early as Friday! My doctor has to release me, but the therapists have all agreed I'm ready."

"Have you called Rob?"

"Of course. But I didn't call Daddy yet. He has the kids this morning, and I don't want to say anything to them until I know for sure, okay?"

"Not a problem. I'll tell him later. I'm so happy for you, sweetie."

As she replaced the receiver and jumped from her seat, Molly let out a loud yes! She ran out of her office to tell Amy the news. "Yes! Yes!"

Molly met Travis and the children for lunch. She finally had a moment to share the good news when the kids ran to play on the climbing equipment. "Travis?" she reached for his hand. "Laney's coming home." She filled him in on the details.

Tears welled up in his eyes.

"I can't explain," he choked. "I better leave before the kids see their old grandpa falling apart." He leaned over and kissed Molly hard. "I am the happiest man on the face of the earth!"

Molly's heart swelled with Travis' display of emotion. She watched as he tapped on the side of the spaceship slide and waved good-bye to his astronaut grandchildren inside the plastic bubble.

Hunter and Ellie came readily when she called them a few minutes later to leave so they would have time to color Easter eggs with their mother and Eli. Road construction made the five-minute drive drag on.

"Grams, tell Hunter to stop making faces at me!"

"I'm not making faces. She keeps trying to take my book."

"Do not!"

"Do, too."

The volume increased with each accusation. Molly couldn't stand it. "Ellie, let your brother read his book. Hunter, don't make faces at your sister."

"I didn't!" Hunter complained.

"Did, too!" Ellie was back in the fray.

"Okay. I can't listen to this. Don't look at each other or say another word. You want to dye Easter eggs, don't you?"

Molly took in a deep breath, turned on the radio, and tuned the children out. She refused to let them dampen her spirits. Laney would soon be home. Lissa would soon be engaged. Her daughters were happy. It would take more than a third grade/kindergarten feud to bring her down today.

"What's that song, Grams?"

Molly thought a moment about the song. She turned the radio off and tried to think of something to distract her grandchildren.

"Hey, look. The traffic is moving again. We'll be there in no time!" Molly exclaimed. She looked in the rearview mirror. It worked. Hunter and Ellie strained in their seatbelts to look ahead.

Eli was waiting by the elevator when they finally arrived at the rehab unit of the hospital. "Come on, guys!"

Ellie and Hunter bounced down the hall beside him to the Dubois Family Life Center. Laney was already in the kitchen. She had boiled the eggs and readied the dyes in an assortment of small bowls on the table. Each of the children picked up an egg. Ellie immediately plopped her egg in a bowl of red dye. Eli picked up a white wax crayon and made designs on his egg. Hunter followed his new mentor, writing his name on his egg with the wax crayon before dropping it into the blue dye.

Forty minutes and two dozen eggs later, the children helped clean up the area without being asked. Laney insisted her mother sit down while she washed the bowls in the warm, sudsy water she had prepared in the dishpan.

"Have you ever noticed how comforting it is to wash dishes by hand?"

"I had the same thought not all that long ago," Molly admitted. "Though I remember a time when you considered doing the dishes a punishment. It's funny how we change."

"I know I've changed. I'm still changing."

She thought Laney meant more than the physical changes she had undergone. Shouts and laughter kept her from asking about it, though. Hunter, Ellie, and Eli were rough-housing in the living area.

Before Molly could say or do anything, Laney took charge. Her voice carried the authority of a mother who meant business.

"This is not a playground," she announced. The three stopped. She gave Eli a carton of the decorated eggs, shooting her own children a look that warned them not to claim it unfair that he got half of their creations. Eli set the carton of colorful eggs on his lap and prepared to leave.

"When you come back, come to my room, and I'll show you the video game my dad brought me," he told Hunter. As he wheeled his way down the hallway, Laney led the way back to her own room.

"How's his mother doing?" Molly asked.

"Not great. I keep hoping your paths will cross. She needs a friend."

"Don't we all," Molly murmured to no one in particular.

Molly lay in bed, the soft comforter pulled over her. Travis kissed his wife on the forehead gently. "Good morning. Do you know what today is?"

Molly sat up and glared at the clock. She had overslept. Lissa and Mark had arrived late in the night. Molly and Travis had stayed up to greet them, then fallen wearily into bed. Rob and the children spent the night at their own house. Afraid they wouldn't be able to sleep, he had decided to wait until breakfast to tell the kids their mother was coming home.

Lissa and Mark were in the kitchen making pancakes and sausages by the time Molly dressed and made her way downstairs. Travis poured her a cup of coffee.

"I think I could get used to this," Molly remarked. She sat down in her usual spot and put the napkin on her lap. Lissa's huge bouquet of fresh-cut roses had taken over the kitchen island.

Lissa moved three of the long-stemmed flowers into a smaller vase and set them in the center of the kitchen table, bringing a sense of springtime and hope to the setting. From now on, Good Friday would be considered Great Friday by the Tiptons.

This was the day Laney was coming home.

Mark poured warm syrup on his pancake. "What time will she be released?"

"Rob thinks around ten or so. I'll go with him to drive his car back. He's going to come home in the van with Laney," Travis answered.

"Whose van?" Lissa asked.

Molly picked up the tub of butter. "It's a public transportation van for people in wheelchairs." She still found it difficult to use the word *handicapped* when speaking about her daughter, even though the van was part of the HATS program—Handicap Accessible Transportation Service.

Lissa cut into a sausage. "I can't wait. What's the plan?"

"Tammy's going over to the house to stay with the kids. Rob will come here and pick up your dad. I made chicken salad and cut up some fresh fruit last night, and I have hot dogs for the kids. We'll pick up some buns and fresh croissants to make sandwiches. I figure Laney will get home around lunchtime."

"Mark and I can pick up those things. I need to stop by the store anyway. I want to get one of those cakes from the store bakery."

"That's a great idea," Molly agreed. "Get enough for all of us, plus Tammy, Andrea, and Evan."

Lissa nodded. The plan in place, the four adults ate their breakfast.

"Mom, Dad, I was going to tell everyone this on Easter, but I don't want to wait." She looked up at her parents. "Mark asked me to marry him, and I said yes."

A wide smile spread across Lissa's face. Molly and Travis stood to hug their daughter. Travis shook Mark's hand.

Molly offered him a warm embrace. Then, she held her daughter close. "Honey, I am so happy for you."

"I wondered last night if you had asked her yet," Travis said to his future son-in-law.

"When are you going to tell Laney?" Molly asked.

"Sometime this weekend. I don't know. This is a big day for her. I don't want to steal her thunder."

Of course.

Mark had told Lissa of his clandestine meeting with her parents. Travis and Molly now offered their version of the evening at the Thai restaurant.

"We've talked about possible wedding dates, but I wanted to make sure Laney was okay first," Lissa shared. "I'm thinking, I mean, *we're* thinking, maybe October?"

"October! That's less than six months away!" Molly exclaimed. There would be so much to do, so many details to plan.

"Don't worry, Mom. We just want something simple."

Something simple had a way of turning into a lot of work for the mother-of-the-bride all too quickly. She remembered how Laney had insisted hers was a simple wedding. The big elements were simple. The cake, the dress, and flowers were no problem. The wedding was at their church with a reception at the community center. The first snag came with the hiring of a photographer. Then the caterer they wanted didn't have their selected date available. Laney added a limo to the list, a live band for the reception, a soloist from the conservatory of music, and hundreds of candles everywhere.

Molly bit her tongue. She would do what she could. In truth, the idea of planning a wedding seemed to be a welcome change from the last few months of constant worry.

She only wondered what Laney would say.

Chapter 21

AT NOON, MOLLY SUGGESTED HUNTER and Ellie eat their hot dogs on the front porch so they would be the first ones to see their mom come home. Forty minutes later, Tammy, Lissa, and Mark joined the kids, all turning their heads each time a car came down the street.

"Rob called," Molly reported to the crew. "They need one more signature to leave the rehab center." The wind caught the welcome home sign the children made, ripping it loose from the railing. Hunter's shoulders sagged.

"That gives us time to fix this sign," Lissa said. Tammy stood to help, but the children sat like guards at their posts.

A movement caught Molly's eye. Parked on the other side of the street in front of a brick house was a silver car. The woman behind the wheel was the same one who seemed to be always lurking about. *So that's where she lives.* The car started and pulled away.

Andrea and Evan had arrived around one. Now as two o'clock was quickly approaching, Molly considered pulling the food out for everyone.

She set plates out and was about to retrieve the chicken salad from the refrigerator when the scrambling of feet and squeals of "Mommy's home! Mommy's home!" pierced the warm April air.

Molly's heart skipped a beat. She raced outside.

Travis, in Rob's car, was close behind the van. He pulled up to the curb and jumped out. The driver of the van lowered the lift bearing Laney. She sported a dark green warm-up suit, her hair pulled back in a ponytail. Pinned to her jacket were pink carnations.

"Look at you!" Lissa cried. "You even have a corsage for homecoming. Rob, you are such a romantic."

Rob grinned.

The group made their way up the ramp, Ellie and Hunter bouncing ahead. Laney suddenly turned her chair around on the newly renovated porch.

"You built this for me, didn't you, Daddy?" It was more of a statement than a question. Travis hugged her.

A gleeful Ellie pushed open the door. "Mommy, come see our new house!"

Laney pushed her chair inside. She took a deep breath as her eyes surveyed the room. "It's more beautiful than I imagined."

"Show me everything," she said to Evan. "Everything."

Thirty minutes later, the group gathered in the kitchen area enjoying chicken salad and fresh fruit. Molly made sure everyone had a drink, napkin, and refills.

"Well, this seems like as good a time as any," Lissa said, looking at Mark. The room fell silent. Was it something in her voice, or did Laney and Rob suspect what would come next?

"Mark asked me to marry him, and I said yes."

"I knew it!" Laney threw her arms up to embrace her sister. "I want details."

Lissa started with Mark's covert visit with Travis and Molly.

"Made it through the gauntlet, huh?" Rob said.

Travis acted offended. "Not fair. We aren't that scary, are we?"

Everyone laughed, and Lissa continued. "Then night before last, he gave me fifty red roses and said, 'I want to spend my whole life with you. Here's my down payment on the first fifty years.'"

"Only fifty?" Rob asked.

"That's all I could afford right now," Mark said sheepishly.

"Yeah, but now she'll expect fifty every year," Evan said.

"Not true." Andrea said. "We like flowers anytime. Not only on our anniversary. Right, girls?"

"And he gave me this." Lissa pulled out a small silver locket from beneath her sweater. The front was embossed with a rose, a small diamond mounted on it. "It belonged to his grandmother." She opened the locket. On the right side was a small picture of Mark and Lissa. An inscription on the other side read *Forever.*

"You had it engraved?" Molly asked. "How sweet."

"Actually, my great grandfather had it engraved for his bride. Then my grandpa gave it to my grandmother. My grandparents had six girls. I was the first grandson, so my grandmother said I was to give it to the woman God had chosen for me."

Tammy touched the embossed rose. "Is the locket in place of an engagement ring?"

Lissa nodded. "We're going to get matching wedding bands. We're thinking October." Lissa reached across the table to Laney. "And I want you to be my matron of honor."

Laney bit her lip. "I'm so honored. But . . . are you sure? I mean . . . you know."

"Oh, Laney, you're sisters," Andrea began. "Of course, she wants you to stand up for her!"

Silence. Then Laney started to chuckle. Soon Lissa joined her.

"What? What are you laughing at? What did I do?" Andrea asked.

"Nothing, Andrea. You are just being yourself, and I love you for it," Laney told her. "Most people walk on eggshells around me." Lissa and Laney snickered even more.

"I know what you mean," added Lissa. "It's like they tiptoe around the topic." Laney laughed harder.

"I don't get it," Andrea said.

"Don't worry, Andrea. It was a lame joke." Laney was now almost crying. Tammy, Rob, and Evan snickered. Molly found a smile tugging at the corners of her mouth.

Travis walked out the front door and stood silently by the new porch rail.

Molly followed him.

"I don't think making jokes about Laney being paralyzed is funny."

Molly stood behind him, her hand on his shoulder. "It's not my brand of humor either, but it shows Laney's healing."

Travis seemed to be thinking this over when the silver car slowed in front of the house. The driver stared at them.

"That's the same woman from the other day. The car is different, but it's the same woman," Travis noted.

"I think she lives in that red brick house over there. She was parked out in front of it this morning."

"I don't think so. I met the old man who lives there. He came over one day to "supervise" my work. Rob said his wife died. Besides, I've

never seen either of those cars there in all the time I've been working here."

Molly shifted. Why did she feel so very uneasy?

"Wanna come with us, Mom?" Lissa asked Saturday morning.

"No, you and Mark go on. Your dad's going for a run, and I'm heading to the grocery store."

Molly fought the crowded checkout lines to purchase everything
for Easter dinner. Now that the meal would be at Laney's house, they
decided to keep it easy—a ham, potato salad, and baked beans.

Lissa and Mark would be around only for the weekend. Laney
needed time with Rob and the kids and with her sister. Molly could wait.

In her own kitchen, Molly set to work making a cake in the shape
of an Easter egg. She had made a doll cake for the fifth birthday of each
of her girls. Surely, the process would be similar. Since she didn't have
a cake pan that shape, she started by baking three individual cakes.

Molly cut each cake into the oval shape of an egg in graduating
sizes, stacked them, and attempted to fill in any gaps with icing.

The telephone rang every few minutes. Molly screened the calls
by turning on the speaker to the answering machine.

"Just learned Laney's home."

"So happy Laney's home."

One caller didn't say anything, but Molly could hear someone
breathing. Not hard. Not creepy. Breathing as if uncertain about what
to say.

"Hey, Mom. Just checking in . . ." *Lissa.*

Molly fumbled to hit the stop button on the answering machine.
"I'm here. Don't hang up. I was just icing a cake for tomorrow."

"Yummy. Anyway, I wanted you to know Mark and I brought the kids to McDonald's for lunch. Laney needed to rest."

Molly looked at the clock. 12:45. Where was Travis? He should have been home long before lunchtime. "Thanks. Dad didn't go over yet, did he?"

"Nope, haven't seen him since breakfast. Gotta run. We'll be home later."

Molly looked in the garage. Travis had taken the car, meaning he probably drove to the river trail to run. She called his cell phone but jumped when it rang on the charging station behind her.

The kitchen was a mess. She had bowls of colored icing and pieces of cake trimmings in piles on the table where she had been working.

Travis had left the house over four hours ago. His run usually took no more than an hour, including warming up and cooling down. What if something had happened? He didn't have his cell phone. Did he carry an ID?

Messy kitchen or not, she scrambled to get her shoes on. She grabbed her keys and went to get her own cell phone from its charger when she realized it wasn't there. She dialed her number.

"Hey, Molly."

She slumped in relief. "Where are you? I thought you would be back by now."

"Just running a few errands. Everything okay?"

"Fine. Did you eat lunch?"

"Not yet. Should I pick something up?"

Molly explained that everyone else was cared for and yes, she would love a sandwich.

"By the way, did you realize you took my phone this morning?"

"Well, that explains the calls I've been getting. You were right. We shouldn't have picked out matching phones."

The giant Easter egg cake rested on a foil-covered tray Molly made out of an old cardboard box. She was trying to make pink icing when her grandchildren came bouncing through the door.

"Grams! Look what Uncle Mark got us!" Each held up a colorful kite.

"Wow!" Hunter pointed to the cake. "Is that a model volcano? Cool! Just like my science project."

"Well, it's supposed to be an Easter egg cake," Molly said in a small voice. "But it's not as beautiful as I imagined."

"I like it," declared Ellie. "Can we decorate it?"

Molly sighed. "Sure, why not?" She put the bowls of icing and two soft, rubber spatulas in front of the children and left the two artists alone to decorate the hideous egg.

Molly stopped the hair dryer. "I should have made arrangements to help Laney get ready for church. Or at least help with the kids."

"They'll figure it out, Molls," Travis said.

Molly abandoned their traditional Sunday fare and set out a bakery pastry for breakfast. She made a pot of coffee and while it brewed, put the ham in the oven and the beans in the slow cooker. Soon, Lissa, Mark, and Travis joined her.

"I think this is the first Easter I didn't get an Easter basket from you and Dad," Lissa said.

"Don't speak too soon." Travis got up from the table and disappeared into the garage. He returned with two potted lilies—one for Lissa and one for Molly.

"I got one for Laney, too."

He winked at Molly and then held up a finger. "Wait, there is more." He headed back to the garage and brought back a box of chocolate peanut butter eggs and two cards. He handed the cards to Molly and Lissa. He gave the candy to Mark. "You better share these, my friend."

Molly and Lissa opened the Easter cards and read the long messages Travis had written inside each. Both women smiled and sniffled as they read the heartfelt words from husband and father.

Molly threw her arms around Travis even as Lissa was heading toward him with open arms.

The church traditionally offered three services on Easter morning. If the weather was warm enough, the sunrise service was held outside. The second and third services featured the choir and drama team.

As the Tiptons pulled into the parking lot, it was clear advertising for the Easter cantata had been successful. Travis dropped his passengers near the front entrance before finding a place to park at the rear of the building. Lissa and Mark stepped inside while Molly waited for Travis on the front portico of the church.

"The Camdens aren't coming," Lissa reported as Travis walked up the walkway. "Laney just texted me back."

"Maybe that's just as well," Travis noted. "This is an awfully big crowd."

Travis was right. It was so crowded, there was a moment Molly felt claustrophobic. How would Laney feel in her wheelchair with everyone pressing in on her?

Still, if only they had called . . .

Molly took a deep breath. She would enjoy this morning with her family. She would not spend the next hour thinking about all the What Ifs in her life.

They found a row of seats and scooted toward the middle. Molly looked around. Andrea and Evan were seated two rows ahead of them. The young couple had become regular attenders.

The room darkened, and the spotlight opened on the choir. In the final act, the empty tomb was revealed. The auditorium lights came on. The audience was invited to stand and sing the chorus of "He Arose" with the choir.

Pastor Haynes moved to center stage as the congregation sat. Molly tugged at Travis' sleeve to see his watch. Surely, Pastor Haynes wasn't going to preach a whole sermon after the cantata.

"Easter is not about Easter egg hunts. Although . . . " He held up an Easter egg. "In most parts of the world, the egg is symbolic of a new life. New life is what Easter is about. Jesus dying for us is in itself worth celebrating. But it is the resurrection that separates us from everyone else. Jesus died. But Jesus lives!"

The congregation clapped.

Pastor Haynes held up his hand. "I don't want us to leave this place today saying, 'What wonderful music.' I want us to leave this place saying, 'What a wonderful Savior.' I'm going to ask the choir to sing that last song again. If you want to make that song your theme song today—if you want a new life—then I'm asking you to meet me here at the front."

Molly reached for her purse, ready to leave as soon as the song ended. Travis squeezed her arm. She turned back around in time to see Andrea and Evan scooting past others in their row toward the aisle. *They're anxious to leave, too.*

Evan and Andrea walked down the aisle toward Pastor Haynes.

Oh. Deep conviction squeezed her heart. She'd been in such a hurry to leave—what else had she missed?

Chapter 22

MOLLY LONGED TO CARE FOR Laney once she was home.

"I don't need a babysitter," Laney insisted. Still, Rob stayed home on Monday. On Tuesday, he stayed long enough to get the kids on the bus, then headed to work.

"I'll be fine," she told her mother on the phone. "Beverly's bringing lunch, and dinner will be easy. I'm making ham salad out of the leftovers."

She would drop by after work anyway. Maybe even help with dinner.

"How was your visit with Beverly?" she asked.

"It wasn't exactly a visit. She brought a directory of services I might need. I showed her everything Evan did. She may call him to take a look at her place."

Tour the house? Was that all they did? She could hardly ask about the Bible study they seemed to enjoy together. Laney had never mentioned it. What was Beverly's house like? Who helped her when she had her accident?

" . . . bring her husband and kids over Thursday," Laney was saying when Molly pulled her mind back into the conversation.

Should she really be sitting here talking when there was so much to do? Perhaps she should pick up her granddaughter. She looked at her watch. "That's nice. Did you take your meds today? Should I go get Ellie? And maybe I could throw a load of laundry in for you while I'm here."

"Yes, I took my meds. Rob is picking up Ellie, and I doubt there's much laundry."

"Well, how can I help you?"

"Mom, you don't have to work every time you come over. It's fine to just sit and visit."

"But I like helping you. I feel useless coming over and doing nothing."

Laney sighed.

Wednesday, after work, Molly brought Laney cereal. "They had the cereal two for one; plus, I had a coupon, so I got a box for the kids."

On Thursday evening, Travis and Molly dropped by with pie and ice cream. A van was parked in the driveway.

"Looks like they have company," Travis said. "Did Laney know we were coming?"

"Of course. I come every day. She'll think I abandoned her if I don't show up."

"Molls, you can't be checking up on Laney every day."

Molly was already out of the car and headed up the ramp. "It's all right. She expects me." By the time Travis reached the ramp, Molly had opened the front door.

"Hey, sweetie! I—I . . . " Molly stammered when she saw Beverly and her husband in the living room. "I'm sorry we didn't call. I didn't realize you had company. I'll just put this in the kitchen, and we'll clear out of your way."

Laney had actually said something about them coming over, hadn't she?

"That's silly, Mom. Stay. Beverly's more like family, anyway."

Derrick shook Travis's hand. "Rob tells me you did a lot of the work on the house. It's great."

"We all worked on it. The contractor was the real force behind it, though."

Squeals and the beating sound of running feet interrupted the conversation. Three little girls raced down the stairs, Ellie in the lead.

Beverly intercepted them at the bottom of the stairs. "Tasha! Tiara! You stop that runnin' and hollerin'!"

"We're monsters," Ellie explained. "Tiara got scared."

"Well, stop it," Laney said. "Maybe you could play with your dollhouse."

Laney made coffee, and the adults indulged in Molly's cherry pie and ice cream. The kids ate the ice cream. Even Hunter emerged from his room to enjoy a dish.

"He's overwhelmed with all the girls," Laney explained as Hunter rushed back up the stairs.

In response to Rob's questions, Derrick filled them in on the costs for a fully equipped van. Molly only halfway listened while she cleaned up the remnants of the pie and ice cream.

" . . . so Laney could drive herself back and forth and not depend on HATS," Derrick said.

Laney getting behind a wheel again? Molly shuddered. Absurd! She rinsed the children's bowls and slid them into the dishwasher.

What did Laney say? "Are you planning to go back to work? I mean—soon?" she asked.

"Of course. You knew I helped with some of the files even while I was in rehab. Anyway, Michelle and I talked about me working a few days from home . . . "

Oh, work from home. Good.

"And some days in the office."

"That's great!" Travis stirred cream in his coffee. "Some companies wouldn't let you do that."

"Laney's good. They don't want to lose her," Rob said.

"I say, go for it, girl," Beverly added. "And the sooner, the better. You gonna go crazy jus' sitting around all day."

"Laney was in the hospital and rehab for nearly three months. She can't just jump back into work." Molly sat down on the arm of the sofa.

"Beverly works, Mom."

Molly shot a glare at Beverly. "True. But you didn't have kids when you had your accident, right? I think Laney needs to stay here and take care of the kids and get her life together before she tries to go out and conquer the world."

"Mom!"

"What I think is that it's time for us to clear out of here." Travis retrieved Molly's sweater from the back of the couch. "Derrick, it was nice to finally meet you. Let me know if you decide to renovate. I'd be happy to help." He headed toward the door. "Molls?"

She wasn't ready to end this conversation, but it didn't appear she had a choice. She mumbled a goodbye and followed Travis out the door.

"Why are you so upset?" Travis asked once in the car. "You should be happy everything is getting back to normal."

"Normal? What is normal? She can't keep up with everything at home as it is. How will she be able to work?"

"They can get someone to help with the house."

"So, let me get this straight. Laney goes to work so she can earn enough money to pay someone to clean her house so she can go to work. What's wrong with just working from home part-time?"

Travis pulled in a deep breath and blew it out. He leaned his elbow on the car door as he drove.

"You can pull away as far as you like, Travis Tipton, but you know I'm right."

At home, Travis retreated silently to his man cave, and Molly turned on the television in the family room. *Why am I always the "bad guy"?* It had always been that way. Travis would bring home candy. Molly served vegetables. Travis would play. Molly made the girls take a bath. Maybe she came on a bit strong, but she knew what was best for Laney.

When she stopped by the Camdens' on Friday afternoon, Molly apologized for her outburst on the previous evening.

"I hope I didn't offend Beverly. It's just that her situation is so different from yours."

"Beverly was fine. After you left, she explained that your reaction is normal."

Heat rushed to her face. "My reaction?"

Laney ignored her. "I'm getting someone to come in one or two days a week to help with light housework when I start back to work."

"Why spend your money like that, Laney? I don't mind helping you when you're ready to get back in the swing of things."

"But, Mom, you work all day, and I'll be working. We don't have the stairlift installed yet. I can't imagine what the kids' rooms look like."

"I'll check their rooms now." Molly headed up the stairs. Surprisingly, Hunter's bed was made and the toys put away.

Ellie had attempted to make her bed, but the spread was lopsided, causing it to pool on the floor on one side and barely cover the mattress top on the other side. Molly straightened the sheets and spread, picked up a few toys, and snagged a brown apple core from the nightstand.

Peeking into the room that had once been Laney's, Molly discovered Rob had moved a desk and chair into the room. The medical bills were no longer piled on the floor. She put her hand on one of the desk drawers but stopped short of opening it. *I'm too nosey.*

She closed the door and headed downstairs.

Laney was talking to someone. Molly was startled to walk into the living area to find a young Hispanic woman sitting on the couch.

"Mom, this is Marisol. Marisol, this is my mother."

"Nice to meet you." Molly smiled.

"Marisol will be coming in to help with the housework. I hope you left something for her to do."

This was moving fast. Laney wasn't going to discuss it. She had made up her mind. Strong, willful Laney. The same Laney who got them in this mess. Doing what she wanted instead of putting her family first. "Humph!"

"What did you say, Mom?"

Molly turned to her daughter and said rather coldly, "Nothing."

Marisol left, and Laney retrieved two bottles of water from the refrigerator. "Is the upstairs a nightmare?"

"Not really. Actually, better than I expected. I put most of Ellie's heavy winter stuff up in the top of her closet."

"Thanks, Mom. Look, I know you don't approve of me going back to work. I promise if it gets to be too much, I'll scale it back, okay?"

"I know. It's just that I have been around long enough to see the big picture. You . . . "

"Mom," Laney interrupted, "let's not go there. Not today, okay?"

Molly took a drink of her water.

An uncomfortable silence stretched between them.

"Laney, on a different subject, do you know the people who live in the brick house with the dark brown trim?"

"The two-story? That's the Albright house. His wife died a few years ago."

"I saw a woman in a car parked there. Maybe it was his daughter. How old is he?"

"Ancient. But they didn't have any kids. In fact, Rob said Mr. Albright may sell his house and move into one of those assisted living places."

"It was a silver car and a woman about my age."

"Maybe it was Nancy."

A cold chill shot through Molly. "Nancy?"

"Nancy Peters. She lives a block over. The realtor? I bet she's listing the place for him."

"Maybe." She finished her water. The uneasy feeling clung to her. It wasn't Nancy Peters. Molly was more certain than she wanted to be.

Molly set the plates on her own kitchen table later that evening. "It was Nancy Johnson, Travis. I know it was."

"Nancy Johnson was plump and had jet black hair."

"So, she lost weight. Dyed her hair."

"You haven't seen Nancy Johnson since Laney's wedding, what, ten years ago?"

"You're probably right. When Laney said Nancy, I may have let my imagination go wild."

Molly was hanging up Travis' jacket later that evening when she discovered the plastic grocery bag on the floor of the hall closet. The forgotten chocolate bunnies.

Giving the candy to her grandchildren wouldn't be a problem. In fact, it would give her another good excuse to stop by their house. She could give Travis his rabbit any time. Eli was the issue. When she purchased the candy, she thought she would see Eli at the rehab center on Easter Sunday. Then Laney had been released, and Molly never again thought about the chocolate bunnies or Eli. *Next week.*

"Look what the Easter Bunny left for you, Travis Tipton." Molly hopped the cardboard and cellophane box across Travis' chest as he lay stretched out on the couch.

"Hey, I loved these as a kid! I saw they were half price now. I was thinking the other day I should get one."

The smile on Molly's face fell. "I bought it before Easter. I just forgot about it until now."

Travis thought she purchased the candy on sale. If she took it to Eli, would he think she was cheap? She wanted him to realize how thoughtful she had been. She wanted him to say something like, "Laney's mother is really nice."

Saturday, when Molly called Laney to say she had made roasted chicken and pasta salad, Laney apologized. She'd invited Andrea over to help her plan for her return to work on Tuesday.

"I'm sorry, Mom. I didn't know. Andrea and Evan are staying, and we're grilling out."

"Don't worry about it," Molly said, swallowing her frustration. "It was just an idea. Daddy and I'll see you tomorrow." Molly gritted her teeth as she replaced the receiver.

Left out of Laney's life again.

Travis loaded his plate with a second helping of pasta salad. "You're overreacting."

How could a man be so sensitive and sweet last week and so obtuse now? Screaming was not an option. Molly set her jaw and started to clear the table. If Travis wanted thirds, let him get them from the refrigerator himself.

Sunday was no better. Laney and Rob didn't come to church. The children weren't there.

The kids were happy when Molly showed up on Monday with their chocolate bunnies.

"I've picked out two outfits for my first day back at work, but could you help me decide which is best?"

Molly helped with the outfit but nothing more. She offered to dust, but Laney said no.

"I have Marisol coming on Friday, remember?"

"Well, at least let me make your back-to-work dinner."

"Pork chops and scalloped potatoes?"

Finally. Something she could do.

Chapter 23

LANEY CHATTERED ALL THROUGH HER back-to-work dinner Tuesday evening. "And they had balloons up and a sign . . . And did I tell you they ordered a special desk for me? I can wheel right up to it."

Molly and Laney cleaned up the kitchen together while the men played a board game with the kids.

"By the way, Mom, I saw that car sitting outside Mr. Albright's house. There was a woman in it, but I couldn't make her out. It wasn't Nancy Peters, though."

"Curious." Could Nancy Johnson be stalking them? Hoping to exact some horrible revenge on Laney?

No. She was doing it again. Letting her imagination get the best of her.

"Rob said it might be the Meals on Wheels people. Nothing to worry about. I'm sure Mr. Albright is okay. We would have heard."

Nothing to worry about. Molly just had to keep telling herself that.

As they left the Camden house, Travis said, "Laney sounded like a girl on the first day of school. And she really appreciated the meal."

"Do you remember her first day of kindergarten? I fixed the very same meal because it was her favorite even then."

Travis chuckled. "I remember. She hardly ate anything because she was so excited about school. She talked nonstop that night, too."

Wednesday's workload proved daunting. During Laney's hospital stay, Molly's colleagues, especially her friend Amy, had teamed together to lighten Molly's load. Now, though, Molly needed to take charge of several projects assigned to her. She needed to meet with a half-dozen clients, three of whom had scheduled phone conferences on Wednesday.

"I'm exhausted," Molly confided in Amy at the end of the day. "And I don't think it's going to get any better." Molly shut down her computer and reached for her jacket. "See you tomorrow, Amy."

Although her plan was to stop by the rehab center to deliver Eli's Easter candy to him, Molly wrestled with herself the entire drive there. Maybe this was a bad idea. Maybe Eli didn't like chocolate, or maybe his parents didn't let him eat it. She hadn't even asked. Would the boy appreciate the gesture? Did it matter? Was she doing this for him or for her?

That was the real question. Being prideful had been a dreadful sin in her childhood home. She should certainly be able to recognize it and put a stop to such selfishness now. Molly turned on the road leading to St. Joseph's.

Nothing had changed, but the music that greeted her, the music that had once seemed so soft and welcoming, now sounded canned and stale. When she made her daily visits to Laney, Molly had barely noticed the green paint on the walls. Now, the hall seemed sterile and empty.

Molly couldn't help but peek as she passed Laney's old room. A man sat in a wheelchair near the window. She moved quickly past the door and into the common room. Eli's room was off the corridor on the other side of the large area. A woman sitting at one of the tables caught Molly's eye. She had dark brown hair and a small cleft in her chin. She looked up to meet Molly's gaze. The blue eyes were the final clue.

"Are you, by chance, Eli's mother?" Molly asked.

A thin smile appeared for a moment on the woman's face. She looked Molly over.

"Yes, do you work here?"

"Oh, no. My daughter was here but went home on Good Friday. Laney. Laney Camden. She kind of looked out for Eli."

"Oh, Laney! Is she okay? She's not back here, is she?" The woman's eyes searched past Molly.

"No, she's fine. I just came to see Eli."

The woman studied Molly's face. She drew back. "Why do you want to see Eli?"

Molly decided to let the awkward moment pass. She sat down in the chair next to the woman, uninvited.

"My name is Molly. Eli is such a sweet little boy. He looks like you. That's how I knew you were his mother." She put the grocery bag with the chocolate Easter bunny on the table in front of her. "I bought him a chocolate Easter rabbit; and, well, then Laney came home, so I forgot about it. I probably should have checked it out with you first, anyway." She pulled the boxed bunny from the bag.

"That was very thoughtful of you. He'll like that. I'm Sarah. Sarah Anderson." Eli's mother now extended her hand and a warm smile to Molly.

"Is he in therapy?" Molly inquired.

Sarah's expression darkened. "No. His father is with him right now."

Molly searched her memory. Had Laney said anything about Eli's parents other than the fact his mother blamed herself? Were they divorced or separated? Molly didn't remember Laney saying anything about it.

"Oh, I can wait a bit. How are you doing? I mean, I've been where you are, you know. It's hard."

Sarah looked down at the table. "I'm fine." Her voice was unconvincing.

"They have a great coffee shop in the other building. Would you like some? My treat," Molly offered.

Sarah looked down the hall toward her son's room. She looked at her watch, fumbled with her purse for a moment, then agreed to the coffee.

"Did you want to tell them where you're going?" Molly asked as the two stood to leave.

"No need."

Molly began second-guessing her impulsive offer to have coffee with the woman she barely knew. She calculated how long she could give to this unplanned visit before she would have to leave and make dinner for Travis. What could she say to plant the seed for a hasty departure? Still, something inside told her Sarah needed her.

"The coffee called Carmello-something is really good," she told Sarah. "I highly recommend it."

Sarah chose a plain coffee but loaded it with French vanilla creamer. Molly bought two of the warm, freshly baked cinnamon rolls and brought them to the table. "I know these aren't good for you, but one every once in a while shouldn't hurt."

The two ate in silence. Molly felt she should somehow know this woman.

"Sarah Anderson. Now I remember. You write a column in the county newspaper. I knew you looked familiar."

"The history column."

"I met you once when they had that tour of historical homes in the area. I think my daughter Lissa went to school with one of the Andersons."

"Lissa?"

"Well, her name is Melissa. Melissa Tipton, but we call her Lissa. She went to school with a Jennifer Anderson."

"Jennifer's my oldest. We had two girls two years apart, Jennifer and Carly. Eli came along ten years later." The two sat in silence for a moment, sipping their coffee.

"We talked of trying for a boy at one time," Molly shared.

"We hadn't exactly planned to have more children. But he's been a joy. He's always been so active; even in the womb, he wouldn't keep still. Wild and rambunctious!"

"He's a great kid. He helped my grandson learn multiplication. Who knows, maybe he'll grow up to be a math teacher. Laney says he's a natural."

"He wanted to—I doubt he'll be able to be an astronaut now." Sarah stared down at the table.

"Eli will get through this. So will you." Molly chose her next words carefully. "I've been where you are, you know. I mean, as mothers, we want to fix everything. And we tend to blame ourselves."

Sarah looked up. "You blame yourself for what happened to Laney?"

"I did. I kept thinking if I had said something or done something differently . . . I don't know."

"I thought Laney was in a car accident."

"She was. But—it's complicated." Molly hesitated. Did she dare betray Laney to this woman? "Should we head back?" The two women left the coffee shop and made their way down the long corridor to wait for the elevator.

"Laney went out to eat with college friends. After dinner, she and another woman went to a bar. They had a couple of drinks. She wasn't charged with anything, and there was ice on the road, but . . . well, the alcohol didn't help."

"It's not the same. Laney is an adult. How could the choice she made be your fault? You didn't tell her to go out for a drive."

"No, but I think about all of the things I could have said or done. I never approved of her friendship with this other girl, and I never approved of her drinking. I let her know it, too." Molly looked at Sarah as they boarded the elevator.

"Don't you see?" Molly said. "Maybe if I had been more approachable, she may have listened to me more in college."

"So, you still blame yourself for what happened to Laney?"

"I think I could have changed some things. But I've forgiven myself." Molly mulled over her own words. She was right. She had forgiven herself. When had that happened? She was about to say something when the elevator doors opened. Sarah stepped off and turned to face her.

"But did your husband blame you?" Before Molly could respond, Sarah turned and headed down the hall.

Molly stood speechless.

She watched as Sarah walked all the way down to the family life center. Molly looked at the plastic bag in her hand. She crossed the common area and made her way to Eli's room, silently praying Mr. Anderson wouldn't be there.

"Hi, Mrs. Tipton! How's Laney? And Hunter and Ellie?"

"Everybody is fine," Molly assured Eli. "I just stopped by to give you this." She handed him the boxed bunny.

"Cool! Thanks!"

Eli's happiness was contagious. She entered the room feeling down but left with renewed energy. She hurt for Eli's mother. Once on the elevator, she turned as the doors closed and caught a glimpse of Sarah heading back through the common area toward Eli's room.

"If someone ever needed prayer, it's that woman," she said out loud.

Chapter 24

MOLLY COOKED DINNER THE DAYS Laney worked. She straightened the children's rooms and did other chores.

In the beginning, Laney seemed grateful for the help; but after a couple of weeks, she complained. "I'm sorry, Mom, but I feel . . . I feel like you're smothering me."

Why would Laney say such a thing? The words cut deep, leaving an open wound in Molly's heart. Was it possible to do too much for the people you loved?

Travis took Molly out for lunch. "You know how independent Laney has always been. Remember when she was two? What was it she always said?"

"Me do it myself." Molly picked at the food on her plate. "I didn't mean to *smother* her. I love her." A knot formed in Molly's throat. Her eyes stung with unshed tears.

"Give her space, Molls. She'll ask for help when she needs it. Trust me."

Molly swallowed her pride, though it was hard to get down, and backed off. Laney wasn't a two-year-old anymore. She was a competent adult. Leave the house to her and Marisol.

There were other issues to overcome. Soon it would be summer. Molly broached the subject with Lissa during one of their daily phone conversations.

"What should we do about the kids this summer?" she asked her younger daughter.

"What do you mean, Mom?"

"School will be out the first week of June, and I'm wondering what to do about the kids during the summer months."

There was a long pause before Lissa spoke. "I think Laney and Rob will figure something out. Maybe they'll enroll them in the YMCA day camp like they did last year."

"But this year's different," Molly argued. "I mean, they've had so much change this year."

"Maybe that's why it's good to get back to normal. You know, treat this summer like every other one."

Normal? Why did everyone seem to think anything could ever be normal? What was normal?

"Mom? Are you there?" Lissa asked. "I don't want to sound mean, but you can't control everything."

Molly chewed her lower lip. *Don't get upset. Change the subject.* "By the way, do you remember Jennifer Anderson from high school?"

"Jenn? Sure. I think she got married and lives in Arizona. Why?"

"I met her mother the other day. Remember Laney talking about the little boy who fell in the barn? That's her brother. I feel so sad for his mom. She blames herself."

"You moms! Always taking everything on yourselves!" Lissa may have been trying to sound light, but the truth of the comment hit Molly hard. Molly frowned as the conversation ended. She ventured down to Travis' man cave and curled up on the couch. Lissa thought she was interfering. But Lissa wasn't a mother yet. She couldn't possibly understand Molly's need to care for her daughter. She couldn't understand Sarah Anderson's deep sense of guilt and how Eli's father continued to feed it.

"You can't fix everything," Travis told her later that evening. "And Lissa's right. Laney and Rob will figure out what to do this summer. I told you, if they need our help, they'll ask."

"I wasn't trying to *fix* anything." Molly tugged at a knot in the yarn with her crochet hook. "I was just trying to look ahead."

"Let go, and let God." Travis headed toward the basement door.

Ugh! What was that even supposed to mean? Let go, and let God what? Let God take care of the kids two days a week while Laney was at work? Let God explain to Hunter why he couldn't be in Little League because Mommy couldn't drive him? He'd already missed out on the YMCA swim team. Everyone had been so busy getting Laney home and settled in, Rob didn't make it to the parent meeting. Let God fix that!

Maybe God gave kids grandparents, so He didn't have to do everything Himself. Did Travis ever think about that? Everyone seemed to think Molly was interfering. Smothering. Fixing. Nobody appreciated her. Her shoulders tensed. She tossed the crocheting aside and headed upstairs.

Molly ran a hot tub of water, rummaged through the assortment of hair products, lotions, and supplies she had shoved into the small cabinet under the sink. Finally, she found a half-used bottle of bath salts one of the girls had given her. She poured the entire contents of the bottle into the running water. The lilac smell was almost overpowering, but soon, she was covered with the hot, scented water. She closed her eyes and tried to relax.

The water cooled, but Molly's disposition didn't. She fed the pain, reliving every comment Laney, Travis, and Lissa had made. The people closest to her seemed to be the least understanding. She pulled on her nightgown. She didn't say goodnight to Travis. She climbed into bed, pulled the comforter and a heavy layer of self-pity over her, and cried herself to sleep.

Travis was already off to work when Molly crawled out of bed the next morning. Lissa called as she downed her second cup of coffee.

"The church is already booked for every weekend in October, so I scheduled our wedding for the last Saturday in September. We'll still have over four months to plan the wedding. I finish my coursework next week, so I'll move home and work on my thesis and the wedding at the same time—I mean, if that's okay with you."

Lissa and Mark arrived on Wednesday night with a rented van filled with her clothes, books, computer, and desk. She'd moved most of the furnishings she had purchased over the past couple of years into Mark's apartment until after the wedding.

Molly looked at her living room, now filled with Laney's dining room furniture, piles of Lissa's bags, boxes of books, and an assortment of storage tubs. She rearranged everything to create a path from one side to the other.

"I'll get this all put away, Mom," Lissa promised. "But first, let's go see Laney. She wants to talk to us about an idea she has."

"What idea?"

"A party! I want to have a party for all the people who helped with the house and everything," Laney chirped as the three sat down at the kitchen table later that day. "I've looked at the calendar, and I'm thinking on Saturday, the twenty-first."

"A party is a big undertaking," Molly warned.

"But Marisol will be here on Friday to clean, and I was hoping you could make your famous brownies. I figure I'll have veggies and dip, and I'll make those little meatballs. We'll need crackers . . . " Laney was in her own world by this time, making a list of party supplies. "We'll keep it simple."

"Sure," Molly answered. "Simple."

"I can make a cheese ball." Lissa took the list from her sister and added other menu items. "And I'll help you decorate. Maybe fresh flowers everywhere."

"I love it! What do you think, Mom?"

Laney and Lissa were on a roll. Molly was tired of being the one putting a damper on everything. "I think it's a great idea. I'll help with the invitations." The three started listing everyone who should be included.

"Mom," Laney began, "does everyone at church know, uh, everything? I mean, about the accident?"

Molly took a deep breath. Laney rarely spoke of the accident. She knew what her daughter was asking. Did everyone at church know that Laney had been driving under the influence?

"Honestly, no one has talked about it to me. Charlie Brown will be at the party, and he knows all of the details; but I really don't know what anyone else knows or thinks."

"I don't remember anything about that night, Mom," Laney whispered. "I mean . . . I know what happened. I just don't remember it."

Molly wished she could wash away the memory of that night as well. She hoped Laney never remembered.

Sunday was Mother's Day. Planning the party with her girls had gone a long way to healing her hurt feelings. But she had given up hope of Laney coming to church, and—in truth—didn't feel much like going to the Celebration Service either. That's what Pastor Haynes had renamed the worship service.

Molly didn't have that much to celebrate.

Lissa left early. Saddened, Molly climbed in the car with Travis. They rode in silence. Her thoughts turned to Mother's Day celebrations of times past. She touched her neckline, remembering the macaroni necklace Laney had made her. Laney had squealed with delight when Molly proudly wore it to church. Still deep in thought, she and Travis arrived, parked a few spaces from Lissa's car and walked into the crowded atrium.

"Here, Mom. This is for you." Molly turned to see her son-in-law holding out a corsage. Behind him stood a smiling Lissa, her hands on Laney's wheelchair.

Molly barely heard any of Pastor Haynes message. She was consumed with the joy of having her whole family with her. She touched her corsage and looked at Laney's. With Lissa's help, Hunter and Ellie had each made a tissue paper flower and fashioned them into a corsage for Laney.

"I got a wonderful book of stories Hunter made in school and a plaster cast handprint from Ellie," Laney said. "Remember the macaroni necklace I made you one year?"

"Funny, I was thinking about that necklace this morning."

Laney touched the tissue paper flowers pinned to her cardigan. "Now I know how much you loved that necklace and why you wore it." Any remnants of self-pity Molly carried with her to church that morning evaporated.

Lissa set up her desk in her old bedroom. She secured a part-time office job filing papers.

Anxious to work on her wedding, Lissa took her mother and sister with her to meet the florist.

"I take it you've picked your colors?" Laney asked.

"I decided the day you came home. Forest green. It's an autumn wedding, and I think green will look great with all the fall leaves and lots of yellow, orange, and red mums everywhere."

They ordered her cake on the next outing. Lissa had a very clear picture of her wedding. Laney and Molly were along for the ride.

"Mark's sister is going to take pictures for us, and I'm making the invitations on the computer."

"What about your dress?" asked Molly.

Lissa looked at Laney, then turned to her mother. "I was hoping I could wear yours."

Molly threw her arms around Lissa. "Yes!"

Molly had saved her wedding dress for her daughters, but Laney had wanted something strapless. Now Lissa *asked* to wear it. Molly's heart was full.

Lissa and Molly spent Saturday morning helping Laney get the house ready for the party. Marisol arrived at the door carrying a covered casserole dish.

"I cannot come to the party, but I made some flan. It is very popular in my country." She handed the casserole dish to Molly. "My brother is waiting for me. I must go now."

Molly put the dish on the counter and kissed her daughters goodbye. "I have to go, too. I have brownies to make. I'll leave you two to finish the decorating."

When Molly and Travis arrived a few hours later, the island was laden with veggies and dip, fresh fruit, Lissa's cheese ball and crackers, and Swedish meatballs. Molly put the brownies on the counter next to Marisol's flan.

By three o'clock, the house was full of people who had painted, hammered, and nailed their way through it for the last several weeks. Laney also invited the women who had provided food for the family and everyone who sent flowers.

Most brought food. Soon the kitchen counters were covered with chips, a variety of desserts, and a big bowl of Charlie Brown's famous homemade trail mix. Only one of Evan's full-time crew members came, but he brought a bucket of spicy chicken wings from a local restaurant, making him a hit with everyone.

Rob got everyone's attention by standing on the stairway. He thanked them for coming and said his beautiful wife had a few words to say. All eyes turned to Laney.

"I . . . I . . . I just wanted to say thank you. I've never felt more loved."

Ellie climbed up on her lap. "I thought you were going to say a speech, Mommy." Everyone laughed.

"We still have a ton of food in here," Rob said. "No one leaves until it's gone!" With that, the party resumed with its light chatter and deep conversations. Molly looked over at Laney, now talking with Deanna, Charlie's wife.

The doorbell rang, and one of the guests moved to open it. Molly didn't recognize the man, but she had not met all of Evan's employees. She returned to refilling the punch bowl.

Laney let out a cry. An alarm sounded in Molly's head. The room grew quiet.

Molly turned to see Rob standing next to his wife, an envelope in his hand. Laney handed a clipboard and pen back to the man. Charlie was already at her side, looking over the papers Rob had pulled from the large envelope.

"Sorry, Mrs. Camden," the stranger said, looking around. "I guess you are having some kind of party."

Laney's face was ashen. Rob looked dazed. Only Charlie seemed to be able to remain calm. He put the folded paper back in the envelope. "Nothing to worry about," he announced to Laney's guests.

But the guests all sensed there was, indeed, something to worry about. They began leaving, and soon the party was only a memory.

A new tragedy had taken its place.

Chapter 25

"I KNEW THAT WAS NANCY Johnson!" Molly was livid.

Once the guests left and Tammy and Lissa took the children to the mall, Charlie addressed the family. "Ten million dollars is excessive, but not unusual."

"We don't have that kind of money," Rob practically growled.

Tears flowed down Laney's face. "I'm sorry. I'm so sorry."

"The Johnsons hold Laney responsible for Tori's death," Charlie explained. "The ten million's a starting point."

"You mean they could ask for more?" Travis asked.

"No. They're indicating how heavily this weighs on them. They won't get that much, but they start high and come down."

"What happens next?" Travis asked.

"First, we answer this summons. Then, we'll file a motion to dismiss."

"So it could be dismissed?" Molly asked.

Charlie cleared his throat. "I don't want to get your hopes up, but that's the process."

"And if it isn't dismissed?" inquired Rob.

"We go into discovery proceedings. That's where we have a chance to hear their witnesses and see their evidence." *What witnesses?*

"Then what? Court?" Laney's voice quavered.

"Judges like to see cases settled out of court if possible. There'll be a pretrial conference first. That's where they lay down the ground rules for the proceedings and give the parties a chance to settle."

The small group was silent. They'd been so focused on getting Laney home, they'd effectively set aside the possibility of retaliation by the Johnsons.

Charlie leaned forward. "Look, Laney, we're a long way from seating a jury. Let's take this one step at a time. Don't worry about what may or may not happen."

Easier said than done. Molly couldn't breathe. She rubbed her temples. Pain pressed in on her like a heavy band of iron.

"One more thing. Don't talk about this with anyone." Charlie stood to leave. "I'll get on this Monday morning."

Deanna Brown had cleaned up the kitchen, while Charlie met with the family. Now she joined them.

"We're not leaving here until we have covered this family with prayer," she said.

"Wouldn't think of it," Charlie said with a smile. Deanna put her hand on Laney's shoulder and started praying. Molly couldn't find her voice. Travis and Charlie also prayed.

As Charlie ended his prayer, Rob asked God to help them all through this.

An hour later, Laney hoisted herself into bed. "Will you stay for a while?"

Molly sat on the side of the bed. It was early. Laney was exhausted from crying. The voices of Travis and Rob, muffled by the thick walls of the old house, drifted in and out. Molly didn't need to use her imagination to know what they were talking about.

"Mom, I was thinking . . . If something happened to one of *my* children, ten million dollars wouldn't be enough."

A knot formed in Molly's throat.

Laney closed her eyes. Maybe she could get a few hours of much-needed rest.

No one in the family made it to church on Sunday. Travis and Molly tried to sleep but found none. They talked, prayed, tossed, and turned their way into the early morning hours when Molly finally gave up.

She got out of bed, crept downstairs, and began cleaning the laundry room closet. It was a task she usually put off. Soon, Travis came downstairs, fully dressed. He turned on his computer and began searching the internet to learn more about a wrongful death suit. It was four in the morning.

True to his word, Charlie began working on Laney's case on Monday. Rob and Laney joined him after lunch.

Molly found herself constantly looking at her watch as Mr. Withers droned on about company restructuring. Twice during the afternoon meeting, she checked her cell to be sure she hadn't missed a text. Charlie warned them the process would be a long one, but this first day seemed unending.

Rob came to the house. "The Johnsons are claiming loss of financial support."

"Loss of financial support? We're not talking about a family losing the breadwinner. How does that make sense?" Molly asked.

"Believe it or not, it does," Rob stated evenly. "Mr. Johnson had a heart attack a couple of years ago. Tori paid for lawn service for the summer and snow removal for the winter to help her dad. As their only child, their lawyer says she would have taken care of her parents in their old age."

Travis frowned. "What does Charlie say?"

"He walked us through our options. We're fighting it. We don't have ten million, and, like Charlie said, the blood alcohol levels were borderline. It was mostly road conditions."

"What's next?" Travis asked.

"We have thirty days to file our answer. I don't know about the rest of it."

"You okay?" Molly asked.

"Yeah, actually we're both a lot better now that we talked to Charlie. I guess the other day we were sort of caught off-guard. We decided to approach this as a part of life." Rob stood to leave. "The pizzas should be ready by now. Laney and Lissa were talking about wedding stuff when I left, but they'll be tracking me down if I don't get back with food soon."

Lissa had a notebook with her wedding outlined in detail resting on the desk in her room. She put it aside and let Laney take the lead in planning. She called Laney her wedding planner.

"I know you're doing this to keep Laney occupied." Molly folded a large towel, still warm from the dryer.

Lissa picked up a towel from a pile on the couch. "A wedding is a big project. Laney's been through it before. But, yeah, I guess it started as a way to help Laney keep her mind off the lawsuit."

"It's a great idea; just don't let it become her wedding instead of yours."

"That's like asking me to lasso a freight train and pull it to a stop. But she does have some good ideas."

"Like what?"

"I'm going to get some of those disposable cameras to set out on the tables so guests can take pictures. Laney said we'll buy inexpensive ones and decorate them."

"She *is* creative. Maybe she'll open a business."

Lissa laughed. "She could call it I Do On a Dime."

"Perfect." The two continued to fold the towels.

"Mom, what was your reception like?"

Molly stopped. Her thoughts carried her back to the March day she had married Travis.

"We had cake and punch, like you're doing. And your great aunt Lucy made little rose mints. Oh, and we had nuts out in little glass bowls around the room. I remember because your dad spent the day helping set up the reception hall at the church and neglected to eat anything. During our reception, he kept eating nuts."

"No little rose mints?"

"No. They were beautiful, but pure sugar and not all that minty anyway."

"Did Uncle Max or Grandpa give a toast?"

"I honestly don't remember. I remember us cutting the cake and your dad eating nuts, but I don't remember much else. We didn't have music and dancing like people do today. We kissed, and everyone clapped. And when we got ready to leave, Grandpa gave your dad twenty dollars for gas money. He gave me a going away corsage and ten dollars. Mad money."

Molly reveled in the sweet memory of her parents' generosity and love.

"I remember that story. That's why Daddy gave Laney a going away corsage. Did he give Rob twenty dollars? I mean, with inflation and all, maybe we're looking at fifty or so, huh?"

"Funny. No, I don't think he gave money to Rob or Laney."

"So, what did you spend your mad money on, Mom?"

Molly walked into the kitchen where her purse lay on the table. She opened her wallet and removed a folded bill from a pocket inside. "I saved it for the day I get really mad."

"That's the same money Grandpa gave you? You never spent it?"

"Grandma and Grandpa didn't have a lot, Liss. It was a real sacrifice. They'd already paid for the wedding. I figured if life ever got really tough, I would have ten dollars. But somehow, we've always managed."

Lissa put her arms around her mother. "I love you, Mom."

"Whenever the lawsuit comes up, Laney's voice tenses up," Rob told Molly when she and Travis came with pasta. "I told Charlie to call me at work."

Rob looked out the window where Laney and Lissa were sitting at the table on the deck poring over wedding books. "I had to give him our bank statements and tax returns for the past three years. It's called full financial disclosure. He also took all of the medical bills. Even the ones we haven't paid yet."

The pile of bills on the bedroom floor.

Molly plated the manicotti. Better to stay focused on the job at hand than to say anything else.

"You know, I'm not usually a big fan of wedding talk, but this one's different. All I have to do is ask how the plans are going, and

I can totally distract Laney from thinking about anything else." Rob picked up the salad bowls. "Want me to take these out?"

Molly's parents were buried in a small graveyard established by Molly's great-great-grandfather. The family cemetery had been preserved by the county's historical society and now had its own access road from the main highway. Large trees shaded the fifty or so gravesites.

On Memorial Day, Molly took flowers to the cemetery. She placed a small bouquet on her grandparents' tombstones and arranged another on the headstone shared by her parents.

"I sure miss you," Molly spoke aloud. "If there really is a Heaven, I know you're there, Mom."

If? Had she really said "if?" Her mother would have been appalled. Why had she expressed doubt? Heaven was real, right? God was real, wasn't He?

But wouldn't a real God take over their lives and make everything right again? No. Life went on. What was it Rob had said? He and Laney *decided* to treat the lawsuit as part of life?

Molly needed to make some decisions of her own. She remembered her mother talking about how some people let life sweep them along. They expect God to come to them like a lightning bolt when what they really needed was to seek Him out. *Seek God? It couldn't hurt.*

The third week in June, Charlie reported that the motion to dismiss was denied. He asked Rob and Laney to come to his office to discuss what he had learned from Rhodes, the Johnsons' attorney.

Molly went with them. Laney said it would be good to have another set of ears and easier for her if she had to use a public bathroom or something.

Charlie opened the file. "The River Rats bartender will testify that Tori and Laney were loud and obnoxious the night of the accident. He was going to pull the plug if they ordered another round. Tori was angry and said something obscene to him when he suggested they'd had enough. He claims he offered to call a cab for her, but Laney assured him she could drive."

Molly gritted her teeth. How like Tori to mouth off to the bartender.

"There's more. The bartender says Laney and Tori ordered several drinks, everything from a pitcher of sangria to more potent drinks. He couldn't be sure who drank what, but he remembered both as being inebriated. Here's the rub. All of the drinks that night were purchased on Laney's credit card."

"Is that significant?" Rob asked.

"It could be. Laney, are you fond of any particular drink when you go out?" Charlie asked.

How embarrassing. Molly could see Laney pale. She had grown up in the church with the Browns. Charlie had been one of her Sunday school teachers. Now he was asking her about her drinking preferences. Did he think Laney was some kind of drunk? An alcoholic? What kind of question was this, anyway?

"I don't remember," Laney said.

"Rob, can you shed any light here?"

Rob looked at his wife, then to Molly. He seemed to be wrestling with himself. "Laney doesn't drink often; but when she goes out, she drinks whatever everybody else is having. She likes it all."

Molly cringed.

"I'm afraid that doesn't help much. There are several drinks on Laney's card. Rhodes will suggest Laney had most of them."

"But what about the sheriff's report? I thought the numbers didn't indicate Laney was . . . " Molly hesitated, " . . . drunk."

"The number was borderline. But in a civil suit, the fact the blood alcohol level is elevated is enough to sway a jury. And they have Laney's letter."

"Letter?" Laney asked.

"A letter you sent the Johnsons. In it, you take full responsibility."

"I vaguely remember that," Laney murmured. She looked at her mother.

Molly shuddered. "I'm so sorry. If only I hadn't mailed it."

"You didn't know, Mom." Laney swallowed hard. Beads of perspiration glistened on her forehead.

"It looks bad, doesn't it?" Rob said.

"Let's just say it doesn't look good. But it's not over." Charlie set the file down.

Laney whispered, "Rob?" Her eyes rolled back in her head, and she slumped in her wheelchair.

Molly rushed to her side. Charlie stepped into the outer office. Rob lifted Laney's head; and when Charlie returned with a wet towel, Rob wiped her face with the cool cloth. An assistant brought in a cold cola.

"It's okay, honey," Rob said over and over.

Laney squinted her eyes. "What happened? I heard a train."

"You fainted. Here, drink this. You'll feel better." Molly held out the plastic cup. A few sips later, the color in Laney's face returned.

Rob and Molly helped Laney exit the office and make the transfer into the car. Her face was stained with tears.

Molly sat in the back of the car and willed herself not to throw up.

Chapter 26

MOLLY'S CHEST TIGHTENED AS LANEY'S trembling voice shared details on the phone.

"I woke up, and Rob wasn't here. At first, I thought he must've started a fire in the fireplace. There was smoke everywhere. I could hear Ellie crying for me."

"Oh, honey, it was just a nightmare."

"It wasn't *just* a nightmare, Mom. I've never experienced anything like it. I woke up screaming."

"Do you want me to come over?"

"No. Rob said I should call the counseling center."

The nightmares continued. Laney couldn't sleep. She couldn't work. Lissa stayed with her Thursday afternoon while she napped. Molly cooked a pork roast with dressing in the slow cooker for them. She had pressed hard to do everything for her daughter; but given a choice now, she'd prefer the strong, independent, at-peace-with-herself Laney.

"I don't care what it costs or what we have to do, we're getting the stairlift," Rob told them after dinner. Hunter and Ellie were busy watching a video. "Even if you never use it, Laney, you need to know you could get to the kids. I think that would help you get some rest."

Laney sighed. "The first one we ordered wouldn't work without widening the upstairs hall landing. I wish we were on the same level."

"I could move in with Ellie for a while," Lissa offered. "Maybe knowing I'm upstairs, you could sleep better."

"But you sleep so soundly," Laney said.

"Then Rob can sleep upstairs with the kids, and I'll sleep with you like when we were kids."

"That might help."

"I wasn't serious, Laney!"

"Just for a little while, Liss. Is that okay with you, Rob?"

"I . . . guess." An alarm sounded in Molly's head—Ol' Sarge's warning that meeting Laney's needs could undo their marriage.

Travis stood and stretched. "Sounds like round-the-clock wedding planning to me."

A week later, Molly, Lissa, and Laney moved up and down the aisles of the craft store where they hoped to find inspiration for the reception centerpieces. The store was full of patriotic wreaths and banners.

"Hey, the Fourth of July is coming up. How about a picnic?" Lissa suggested.

Laney moaned. "I'm too tired and grumpy."

"All the more reason to have a picnic. We can have it at Mom and Dad's. Right, Mom?"

"Then do it," Laney barked. She had met with the counselor twice. Her doctor prescribed a sleep aid, but the result was less than satisfactory.

"Laney, you've got to get out of this mood you're in. You've got to work at it. It's not just messing you up. It's hurting your family."

"That's what I do. Hurt my family," Laney cried out. "Don't you get it, Liss? I may be the one in the chair, but our whole family is paralyzed because of me."

Molly looked around the store to see if anyone had heard the outburst.

"What I see, Laney, is my big sister whining and feeling sorry for herself. Poor Laney. You're the one who always says, 'Act happy, and you'll feel happy.'"

Laney set her jaw tight, her mouth pulled shut in anger. She pushed her chair the few feet down the aisle. "I hate this chair! I can't get away from anybody!"

"I'll make it easy for you!" Lissa headed toward the door. "I'll be in the car!"

Laney's psychological pain cut Travis to the core.

"Even if I offered them everything we have in savings, it wouldn't be enough to make the lawsuit go away. But I've been thinking, Molly. There might be another way."

"How?"

"I can't say. Let me work out some of the details first."

A week passed before Travis broached the subject again.

"Rob and Laney don't have enough to appease the Johnsons. We don't have ten million dollars—or even five million, for that matter."

"We don't have one million, Travis."

"We have our retirement money. Not enough for the Johnsons, but maybe enough for Laney, Rob, and the kids." She and Travis hadn't talked about retiring since the accident. The closest they came was a mutual decision to use some of the money they had set aside to fund the remodeling project. Even that had been more of a nod and an understanding.

"I'm listening."

Travis unveiled his plan. Once he had laid it all out, reviewed every detail, and answered all of her questions, Molly was in full agreement. She marveled at her husband's careful planning and generosity.

"Let me make sure I understand. We take our money out of our respective plans as needed," Molly began.

"Actually, I think what I have in my annuity will cover the initial cost," Travis interjected.

"So, you've looked into this?"

"Yes, every day at lunch."

"And you never said anything?"

"I wanted to make sure. I have been praying about it. I wanted to make sure it was God's will. And—I didn't want to disappoint you." Travis reached for Molly's hand. "You've been looking forward to retiring. If we do this, we won't be able to spend our winters in Florida."

"Even if we don't do this, do you think we would go off to Florida now?"

Travis smiled at Molly. "Come with me. I have something to show you."

Evan, Rob, and Travis worked together to widen the upstairs landing. It required moving a wall in the couple's old room. Finally, the new stairlift was installed. The family gathered for the inaugural ascent.

"Me, Mommy!" Ellie called out. "Let me ride it!"

"It's not a ride," Hunter said. "It's for Mom."

"Hunter's right, Ellie. But I think you should each get to try it; what do you say?" Laney suggested.

Ellie squealed with delight.

"Now I'm going to be able to come up and make sure your room is clean!"

Hunter rolled his eyes, threw his hands up in the air and groaned. Everyone laughed at his melodrama.

With the lift finally functioning, Laney was ready to have Rob back as a bed partner. Lissa moved back to her parents'.

"It wasn't all that bad," Lissa told Molly one morning. "In a way, I feel closer to Laney. All I know is I'm glad she's my sister. Have you noticed they haven't missed a Sunday at church since Mother's Day? I think they're searching for answers."

Maybe Lissa was right. Maybe they were searching.

"I've prayed a long time for Laney to seek a close relationship with God," Lissa said.

Seek. Molly took the jug of juice to the table and sat down. "Want some?"

Lissa pushed her glass toward her mother. "I have a new appreciation for being a mom. I mean, Hunter and Ellie are great. But they can be so rambunctious!"

"I know what you mean. They stayed with us for a bit, you know."

"How did you do it?"

"We had prior training with two little girls."

"You're a real comedienne. Anyway, I'm finally back on schedule with my thesis. I'll be upstairs if you need me." Lissa headed to her makeshift office.

Rambunctious. That was the word Sarah Anderson had used to describe Eli. Was he still in rehab?

She met Travis on the stairs and kissed him. He was already showered and dressed.

"That's my goodbye kiss in case you leave for work before I get back down here," she said.

"I think we should present our plan tonight. If we're going to do this, now is the time to act on it."

"We could take them out to eat."

"Let's not turn this into a big thing."

"But Travis, it is kind of a big thing."

Travis set his jaw. "This is from God, Molls. Not from us."

That look on his face! Travis had scolded her. She started to say something, but let it go. She took a longer-than-normal shower, thinking through what he had said. Molly had learned early on to recognize that look. There would be no more discussion.

She could allow that he'd been considerate of her feelings as he hatched this plan before proposing it to Rob and Laney. But what was this business about it being from God? Okay, yes, God had blessed them, but they would be the ones forfeiting their future to help their family.

Lord, help me understand.

Long summer days meant Molly and Travis could eat the spaghetti Lissa made, clean up the kitchen, and still have plenty of daylight to take Rob, Laney, and the kids for a drive in the country.

"So, where are we going?" Laney asked.

"Just follow us," Travis said.

Hunter and Ellie wanted to ride with their grandparents. They drove past the YMCA and turned on Middleton-Westerville Road.

"This is the road my friend Justin lives on," Hunter called out. "Are we going to Justin's house?"

Travis smiled. "Nope."

They made a turn onto Smith Road, then into a gravel driveway leading to a small, white bungalow with dark green shutters. Once parked, Travis jumped out and helped Rob with Laney's chair. The ground was uneven. The two men managed to maneuver the wheelchair onto the sidewalk leading around the house to the shade of a large oak tree in the backyard.

"Well, what do you think?" Travis began scanning the expansive yard. A rope swing hung from one of the massive oaks.

"Can we swing, Grandpa?" asked Hunter, pointing to the rope. Travis nodded, and the children were off.

Laney and Rob quietly took in the old house, small storage shed, and the beautiful property on which the buildings sat.

Travis closed his eyes for a moment. Molly knew he was praying.

"Your mother and I have been asking God to show us how we could help you through the stress of the lawsuit and all."

"You've been an incredible help, Travis," Rob said.

Travis smiled. "We've tried to do what we could. But here's the idea. Why we brought you here.

"This property . . . it's like God had it all worked out. It belonged to the Smith family. When the parents died, the children inherited it, but they don't want it. They heard through someone at church that I was looking for property in the area and decided to sell. For a great price, too. Fifty thousand less than they could get on the open market."

"Why were you looking for land, Daddy?" Laney looked puzzled.

"If your mother and I could, we would just pay off the Johnsons, and you would never have another worry. As it is, you have nightmares about the kids being upstairs, about losing everything. About being homeless."

Laney looked down. Travis knelt in front of her.

He was going about this all wrong. Molly wasn't sure what she would say, but she wouldn't make her daughter cry. And why wouldn't he take credit for what she thought a rather magnanimous act? The only answer she had from her earlier plea to Heaven was to remain silent. Let Travis do the talking.

"You said you had an idea you wanted to talk about," Rob said.

Travis stood. "There's a little more than two-and-a-half acres here. Most of it is just beyond that stand of trees. It's level and prime for building."

"You want to build a house?" Laney asked.

"Well, actually, we're thinking about renovating this old house for us, and you build a house over there. Let Evan design it and build it. We sell our house and use the money to pay for it."

Laney and Rob gazed toward the stand of trees separating the parcel of land. "I don't get it, Daddy. If we lose everything to the Johnsons, we won't have money to build a house."

"That's why I said we'll pay for it. Look, Laney, we paid our house off three years ago. If we sell our place for say, three hundred thousand dollars, Evan could use every dime of it to build a house from the ground up to be exactly what you need. It would be in our name. The Johnsons couldn't touch it. You'd never be homeless."

"They could settle," Rob interjected.

"Then you sell your house and move into your dream house anyway. You can buy it from us when you're ready. Or you can wait around until we kick the bucket and inherit it."

Though Travis laughed, Rob didn't. He seemed to be processing everything. Travis suggested the two men walk the perimeter of the property and discuss the details.

"Would you really want to live in this old house, Mom?" Laney asked.

"After I saw Evan's work, I feel pretty confident he can make this a great place. Your dad brought him out here. He says it has 'good bones.' And we always wanted to downsize once you girls were grown."

"I wonder what Lissa would think."

Molly looked at the old house, with its plank siding. "Well, if we, as your dad says, 'kick the bucket,' this will be her half. We better make it look good."

"I don't know, Mom. I just hate to think of you and Daddy going in debt like this."

"We're not. When all is said and done, we won't owe a dime. Your dad was very clear on that. We'll pay cash for the land and renovations. Then as soon as our house sells, we'll have cash to build your house."

"And if we don't have to sell our house?" Laney asked.

"Then you have a choice."

"It still feels like we're taking advantage of you somehow."

"You would do the same for Hunter or Ellie, right?"

"We would if we could. But I don't get it. Property in this area doesn't come cheap. How could you . . . " Her eyes grew wide. "Your retirement money! We can't let you do that!"

"That's up to us. Don't worry, Laney. As your father says, this plan belongs to God. If it works, it'll be God's doing, not ours." Molly was surprised. She believed her own words.

Travis and Rob returned from their walk and helped get Laney back to the car. Molly and Travis stood in the gravel driveway as they waved good-bye.

"Well, what do you think?" Molly asked.

"I think we should go get some ice cream."

Chapter 27

THE WITNESS DEPOSITIONS FOR THE lawsuit were to begin on the seventeenth of August. Molly met her daughter at a downtown restaurant near Laney's office for lunch the Tuesday before the proceedings started.

Molly ordered a corned beef sandwich and handed the menu back to the server. "We should do this more often."

"I hope we can."

Molly drew in a deep breath. Laney was understandably moody lately. One minute, she talked non-stop about Lissa's wedding; the next, she was quiet and glum.

"I'm sorry, Mom. It's just that I feel like a prisoner on death row, trying to make the most of my final hours. And I don't feel like talking about the wedding."

"Good. Because I feel like that's all we ever talk about anymore."

"Rob uses it to distract me."

We all do. "Then let's talk about something else. Work? Friends?"

"Did I tell you Beverly's no longer my advocate?"

"Oh, no!"

"It's good, Mom. Now we can just be friends. She brought the girls over yesterday after school to play with Ellie. It was so nice to talk about everything. And nothing. You know what I mean?"

"Yeah, I do."

"I told her yesterday she and Derrick need to adopt a boy, so Hunter will have a friend to play with."

"How did that go over?" Molly took a sip of her water.

"Are you kidding? She laughed that big laugh of hers."

"I can hear her now."

The server returned with Molly's corned beef and Laney's turkey sandwich.

"You can say grace, Mom." Laney bowed her head.

Molly closed her eyes. "Thank You, Lord, for Your bountiful gifts. And, God, help us through this. Amen."

If Laney noticed any awkwardness in Molly's prayer, she did not say anything. She began assembling her sandwich, squeezing mayonnaise out of the small, plastic packet. "Did you know Eli went home?"

"No. And I never did get back over to rehab to see his mom."

"Beverly said Mrs. Anderson is a mess, and I guess Eli's dad left them."

Molly dabbed at her mouth with her napkin and took a drink of water. "I knew things weren't good, but I'd hoped it would work out. I know she's still writing her column, though. It's in the county paper."

"The weekly?" Laney asked.

"She writes the historical column."

"I didn't realize that was the same Sarah Anderson. I think Lissa went to school with her daughter. I figured her to be a lot older." Laney stopped. "Sorry, I didn't mean . . ."

"That's okay. I feel rather ancient myself. I wish there was something we could do for her, though."

"Well, there's something I can do." Laney pulled her cell phone from her purse. "I can call her and ask Eli to come over to play. I think we've talked only a couple of times since I've been home, but I'm sure I have her number."

Laney reached Sarah on the second ring. After a few minutes of pleasantries, Laney asked if it would be possible for Eli to come over to play with Hunter. Molly could hear only one end of the conversation, but it sounded like Sarah was agreeable.

Molly smiled at the ease in Laney's voice. She had so much on her own plate, yet she was concerned about Eli and Sarah. Both of her daughters were caring people. Travis used to say they were the founders of The Lost Puppy Club. Only now, the stakes were much higher.

"My mom? I'll ask her." Molly raised her eyebrows. "No, I really can't do that yet. I don't have any transportation." The conversation ended, and Laney turned to her mother.

"Need me to drive you there?" Molly asked.

"No, she's coming to my house. She asked if you were around. She'd love to see you again. She's bringing Eli over around four tomorrow. You available?"

"I should be able to drop by. What was that about transportation?"

"Oh, she just said maybe next time I could bring Hunter to their house. But I don't have any way to do that."

Laney's words lingered as Molly drove home. Before the lawsuit, Laney had talked of getting a specially equipped van. At the time, Molly didn't want to see her daughter behind the wheel of a vehicle again. How foolish. Now she could see how boxed in Laney must feel. She was dependent on everyone. This had to be a tough pill for someone as independent as Laney to swallow. Maybe this was an issue she should bring up to Travis. Then again, maybe not. They couldn't fix everything.

They weren't even sure at this point they could fix anything.

"I love to read your articles," Molly told Sarah the next day. "My mother's family helped to settle this area, so I have always been interested in the history of the county."

"Oh, really? What was the family name?" Sarah inquired with true interest.

"Blevins."

"Of course. I wrote a piece about their farm and the store they ran back in the day."

"Yes! Of course, the farm has given way to a new subdivision now. I was out that way a few weeks ago at the family cemetery."

"I've thought of doing a series on some of those old family graveyards. Maybe we could go out there together sometime."

Eli and Hunter played a video game in the living room. They sounded like two average boys having a great time. Laney poured each of her guests a second cup of coffee.

"Laney," Sarah whispered, "do you think Hunter might be interested in helping celebrate Eli's birthday? It's coming up and, well, he feels a little disconnected from his friends. They're all in sports and everything. I think things will get better when school starts; but right now, he feels friendless."

"That would be great. I'm sure Hunter would love to do that. What did you have in mind?"

"Well, I thought maybe I could take the boys to the Newport Aquarium or maybe just have pizza and a sleepover. I haven't figured it out quite yet."

"Hunter is easy to please. When is Eli's birthday?"

"August seventeenth, next Wednesday. If a weekend works better for you . . . " Sarah's voice trailed off.

Laney's brow furrowed, and her eyes clouded. "We'll see. Excuse me. I better see what Ellie is up to." She crossed over the room to the stairs and positioned herself to get into the lift.

"Was it something I said?" Sarah asked.

Molly paused, considering. How much do you share about family business?

"Remember I told you about the circumstances surrounding the car accident?" Sarah nodded. "Well, there was a passenger. She was killed in the accident, and her parents are suing Laney. The seventeenth is the day they start taking depositions."

"I had no idea," Sarah said.

"It's going to be okay. I don't know how, but eventually, we'll all be able to put this behind us." The two women sat in silence for a moment drinking their coffee.

Sarah put her cup down on the yellow napkin. "Here I've been feeling sorry for myself. You never know how someone else is hurting. You think you're the only one." Sarah spoke quietly. Molly reached out her hand to touch Sarah's, now resting on the table. "My husband, Eli's father, left."

"Are you okay?"

"Angry and hurt. Mostly angry. Striking out and hurting me is one thing, but hurt my child? No way. Eli keeps asking when his dad is coming home. I'm running out of things to tell him."

"So, he doesn't know the truth?"

"Even I don't know the truth. All we know is that he packed his suitcase and walked out the door. He hasn't called or anything."

"Your daughters?"

"They haven't heard from him either. Look," Sarah said, pushing herself away from the table. "I better take Eli home. Tell Laney not to worry about the birthday thing. Maybe I'll try to plan something later."

"I hate to see you go like this," Molly told her. Then to her own surprise, she offered to pray with Sarah. Sarah lowered herself in the chair.

"I can't tell you how long it's been since I prayed," Sarah confessed. "I'm not even sure God wants to hear from me."

"I understand that feeling, but I still think we should try." She bowed her head. She wanted to pray the way Kate had the day she picked up the wheelchair at church. Molly began a simple prayer. "Dear God, please give Sarah strength and help her husband to do what is right and . . . and . . . help this to bring him closer to Sarah and Eli and You. And, Lord, please help Eli, so he doesn't feel abandoned by his dad. And help Eli to adjust to everything. And please let everything work out for Laney, too. Amen."

Sarah squeezed Molly's hand. "Thank you so much."

"I'm sorry. I'm not good at praying a very fancy prayer."

"It was perfect." The two women stood and hugged. Sarah called to Eli to stop the video game. "It's time we leave." They were about to head out the door when Laney returned.

"Sarah, I'm sorry I ducked out on you. Mom may have told you, but I have a few obstacles to get through; and sometimes, I let them overwhelm me."

"You don't need to apologize, Laney." Sarah started to open the front door but turned once more to Laney. "I really do understand. I have a few obstacles of my own."

Chapter 28

THE LAW OFFICES OF JAMES Rhodes were located in a massive granite and glass structure in downtown Cincinnati. It was a good thing Charlie had prepared them for the unbridled opulence—intended to boost client confidence and intimidate the opposition.

The family arrived early enough to find a place to park and get Laney settled in the large conference room. As the defendant, Laney had the right to sit in on all witness testimony. After some discussion, the Johnsons' lawyer agreed Rob could also be present.

"Just listen. Take notes, but don't talk. If you have a question, share it with me and me alone," Charlie instructed.

Charlie had the list of witnesses Rhodes would call. Deputy Steadman wouldn't be present, but his report would be submitted. The bartender from River Rats was scheduled for the morning.

Rhodes also called Gordon Leis. He was the man who came upon the scene and called 911. One of the first responders, a volunteer with the local fire department, was also listed. Both Leis and the firefighter would attest to the smell of alcohol, among other things. Charlie didn't seem worried.

Rhodes had expert witnesses prepared to speak to the issue of driving under the influence of alcohol, Laney's lack of control of the car, and road conditions. There was no question about the weather.

Rhodes, however, would take this tactic to demonstrate they were willing to recognize the conditions were not ideal, but became deadly only because Laney was intoxicated.

Once Charlie, Laney, and Rob were situated in the conference room, Molly and Travis found a couch in the outer office where they could wait. It wasn't an office really, more like the salon of a nineteenth century club. Small sofas and wing-backed chairs were arranged in groups around the room. Molly could picture Sherlock Holmes in one of the overstuffed chairs discussing the merits of Laney's case. She sat down.

"There's a coffee shop downstairs. I'll get us some." Travis wasn't one to sit still.

Molly flipped through a magazine. The massive door opened. "That was quick," she started to say but swallowed her words. Nancy Johnson walked into the room and sat down a few feet away without so much as a glance her way.

"Hello," Molly said.

Nancy Johnson turned in her chair. "Molly." She turned again, so her back was to Molly. Silence covered the room like a dense fog.

"I know we're not supposed to talk," Molly stammered.

"No, we're not."

Molly drew her hand to her mouth and bit hard on her thumb. She didn't want to stay, and she couldn't go. She sat with the open magazine on her lap, the back of a woman who held contempt for her daughter turned coldly toward her.

Molly drew in a deep breath. "Nancy, I want you to know, my heart breaks for you. I can't imagine what you feel."

Silence. *Please, God, help me here.*

"Thank you. Most people say they know how I feel. They don't." Nancy's voice was low but rang like a loud bell in the cavernous room.

Molly chewed her lip. She looked to the door. Her only hope was for Travis to come walking through.

Nancy Johnson continued to face the opposite wall. "My lawyer says Laney doesn't remember that night."

"No, she doesn't remember anything." She could tell Nancy that Laney would be paralyzed for life, but Nancy had been watching them for weeks. She knew—and she evidently felt that wasn't punishment enough. "Is your husband here?"

Awkward silence again filled the room.

"He's in St. Louis General. This has all taken a toll on him." Her voice cracked. She pulled a tissue from her purse.

Molly got up from the chair. Cautiously, she moved to a chair across from Nancy Johnson.

"Oh, Nancy, I'm so sorry. His heart?"

Nancy nodded but didn't look up. "I sent flowers," Nancy said, eventually.

Nancy sent flowers to her husband in St. Louis? So what? Then Molly remembered the mysterious bouquet Laney had received in rehab. *The same flowers as in her wedding.* Tori had been a bridesmaid. Nancy and Paul had driven all the way from St. Louis to attend. "The flowers were beautiful. Just like her wedding."

Nancy glanced up, surprised. "I didn't include a card."

"We didn't know who sent them—until now. Nancy, I've picked up a pen a million times, wishing I knew what to write to comfort you, but the words never came."

Nancy tugged at her tissue. "I always liked Laney."

Molly couldn't say she liked Tori. She didn't. Was this an opening for her to plead with Nancy on Laney's behalf? A paralegal carrying a stack of files walked toward them before disappearing through a paneled door. Molly glanced at Nancy Johnson. The moment was lost. Nancy shifted in her seat and gazed out the window over the Cincinnati skyline.

Molly got up and walked out into the main hallway. She leaned against the marbled wall between the water fountain and elevator and cried.

The elevator opened, and Travis stepped out. He saw Molly immediately. He set the coffee cups in the stainless steel bowl of the drinking fountain. "It's going to be okay, sweetie," Travis whispered in her ear as he held her.

It was a few minutes before Molly regained enough composure to tell Travis what had transpired. The two walked back to the waiting area, but there was no sign of Nancy Johnson.

Almost two hours after the depositions began, Charlie, Laney, and Rob came through the door to the outer office. Travis jumped up to greet them. "What's up?"

"A break of sorts," Charlie told them. "The bartender made his statement; but when we started questioning him, he was all over the place. Then all of a sudden, Mrs. Johnson asked for a break. She said she needed to check on her husband. It seems he is in the hospital."

Molly wasn't sure if she should tell Charlie about her encounter with Nancy or not. She looked to Travis, who seemed to be weighing the pros and cons as well. After all, what could they really add to today's proceedings? That Nancy sent flowers?

"Charlie," Molly began.

"What do you mean the bartender was all over the place?" Travis interrupted.

"I really can't go into details, but he did get confused."

"Maybe they're using this time to practice his testimony," Travis suggested.

"Rhodes can manipulate like the best of them, but he would never coerce false testimony out of anyone," Charlie answered.

An associate summoned Charlie. He excused himself and followed the young man down the wide hallway.

Laney watched. "I wonder what that's about."

"Do you think they could be negotiating?" Rob said. "I mean, that guy's testimony was really questionable. First, he said Tori was the one who was loud; but then later, he said it was Laney. He said he offered to call a cab; but then, he turned around and said he called a cab, but the girls refused to get in it. He's not a credible witness," Rob informed them.

"We're not supposed to talk about specifics of the depositions, Rob."

"I'm just saying." Rob stood up and paced the floor.

"Funny," Laney said, "I hated to see this day come. But now, I just want to get back in there and see it through." She rolled her chair toward the large window. "Mrs. Johnson hates me."

Molly pulled one of the chairs over to where Laney sat looking out over the city.

"She doesn't hate you, Laney. She's just hurting."

"She hates me, Mom. I would hate me, too."

"Laney, remember those flowers? The ones without a card that had all your favorites in one arrangement?"

Laney looked up. Did she make the connection? "Yes."

"Mrs. Johnson sent those."

"How do you know?"

Molly looked to Travis, then back to her daughter. "We kind of had a little talk here before the depositions began. She said, and I quote, 'I always liked Laney.' She doesn't hate you. She just isn't able to forgive you yet."

"I can understand that," Laney whispered.

This was a trial in more than one way, but she had to trust.

They all did.

Chapter 29

"THEY'RE OUT HERE!" HUNTER CALLED. He bounded onto the deck. "We went to the waterpark, and I went down the giant slide."

"I went on the lazy river ride," Ellie added.

Lissa leaned in and kissed her sister. "Mark showed up, so we made a day of it. I had no idea you'd be home this early."

"It's over," Molly said with a smile.

"The depositions?"

"All of it. The Johnsons dropped the lawsuit," Laney told her.

"What? Really?"

"Really," Rob said. "They're settling for what the insurance offered in the first place. And most of that will probably go to paying their attorney."

"I don't get it. What happened?" Lissa sat.

"Her husband was never fully on board, and, well, I think she finally let go of some of her anger. Maybe it was something Mom said." Laney told Lissa about the conversation between Mrs. Johnson and Molly.

Molly shook her head.

"Now what?" Mark asked.

"Now, we all go to our favorite Italian restaurant to celebrate. My treat," Travis said.

Lissa stood. "We have a lot to celebrate. Mark has an interview at the university tomorrow."

"Yes!" Molly and Travis cheered in unison.

"It's just an interview," Mark warned. "These searches take time."

Lissa's wedding invitations were ready to be mailed. Six weeks to the day, she put them together in a large box to take to the post office. "I have some good news."

Molly looked up from the box of invitations.

"Mark's being appointed as an assistant professor at the university."

Molly hugged Lissa. "Oh, honey, that's wonderful."

"We made an appointment with a realtor to look at places Saturday. Want to come?"

"I think not. I'm spending the day with Laney. We have a little shopping to do." They had to scramble to organize a bridal shower.

The Saturday of Labor Day weekend would work best. They bought the invitations and had them in the mail the next week.

"I thought a lot about her shower early on; but with the lawsuit and everything, I sort of let it slide," Laney confessed as they discussed food for the party. With all of Lissa's friends and family, as well as some of Mark's family, the guest list grew to a size too large for either house. Laney secured a room at the church.

Molly unfolded a paper wedding bell decoration. "I invited Mark's parents to spend the whole weekend of the shower with us. It'll be a good time for us to get to know each other. The men can golf on Saturday, and Cincinnati has a huge fireworks display on Sunday night."

The idea sounded great; but as the shower date approached, Molly had misgivings. Laney and Rob invited Mark to move in with them until the wedding. Everything out of Mark's West Virginia apartment had to be packed and moved. Molly referred to her living room as a storage locker.

Mark stacked the boxes. "No need to worry about my parents. They're easygoing, like you and Travis."

Molly didn't feel easygoing. But she did feel good. *There really is light at the end of this long, dark tunnel.*

Red, yellow, orange, and white chrysanthemums filled the church auditorium. Laney rolled down the aisle wearing the dark green gown Lissa had chosen for her. The same woman who hemmed and tucked Molly's dress to fit Lissa perfectly worked her magic on Laney's gown to make sure it looked full and flowing but could not possibly get caught in the wheels of Laney's chair.

Mark's brother was the best man. He met Laney at the front of the auditorium and escorted her up the ramp Travis had built.

Hunter was next, looking very grown up in a tuxedo. As ring bearer, Hunter carried a small chest carved out of wood. He told Lissa he was too old to carry a satin pillow.

Ellie wore a dress like her mother's. She very carefully dropped rose petals as she made her way down the aisle, stopping twice to rearrange the petals so they were evenly distributed. Appreciative chuckles rippled through the audience.

Molly's heart beat hard as the music changed, announcing the bride. She stood and turned, catching only a glimpse of Lissa before everyone else stood. Travis escorted Lissa down the aisle and led her up the steps to Mark.

During the traditional service, they lit a unity candle as Pastor Haynes shared a passage about two becoming one. Mark's sister photographed the key moments.

Afterward, everyone gathered in the fellowship hall for cake and punch. Guests took pictures of each other with the cameras scattered throughout the space. As the newly married couple prepared to leave, Travis approached his daughter.

"I have something for you." He pulled a corsage made of yellow roses from behind his back. "It's a little going away gift." He slipped the corsage over her wrist and kissed her on the cheek.

"Thank you, Daddy. I have a little going away gift for you, too." She turned to Laney, who handed her a small, wrapped package. Travis was clearly surprised. "You can open it after we leave."

The car pulled out of the church parking lot. Travis looked at the gift in his hand. Molly stood by his side and laughed out loud when he opened a package of mixed nuts. The note attached read, "Enjoy your dinner."

Chapter 30

AMY POKED HER HEAD IN Molly's office. "Eating in?"

"I packed, but you're welcome to join me." Molly saved her work and cleared a corner of her worktable.

Amy settled into one of the swivel chairs. "I brought a salad. I'm trying to lose ten pounds before Christmas. Wow, that's beautiful!" She pointed over Molly's shoulder.

Molly turned. "Oh, my screen saver? We took that picture in Florida." Molly considered the sundrenched beach scene. "We wanted to retire there. I put that up when there was still snow on the ground." *I thought a beach scene in February would get me through the month, but then . . .*

"You're too young to be thinking about retiring."

"Not really. Travis will be sixty-one next month, and he can retire when he's sixty-two."

"You would really move away from your girls and the grandkids?" Amy picked up the family photo on Molly's desk.

"We thought we would be snowbirds. You know, live our winters in Florida and summers in Ohio. But now? No."

Amy finished her salad and returned to her desk. Molly stared at the family portrait. Her family. She turned to her computer. The beach scene beckoned her to a desire that now seemed only a figment of her imagination. Retirement? In time. Florida? A distant dream. Molly took one last look at the coastline, then deleted the picture.

The afternoon's work was busy but not hard. After finishing a report and responding to a few urgent emails, Molly reviewed her online calendar for the following week.

"What's this?" she asked Amy. Wednesday, Thursday, and Friday were blocked off.

"That's an administrative block," Amy told her, looking at Molly's computer screen. "You need to ask Mr. Withers, but he won't be back in town until Monday."

Molly checked her project memos. She had no out of town meetings with clients, no conference dates. There was no reason her calendar should be blocked. Three days blocked in a row usually meant a conference or meeting. This could have been planned months ago.

She hadn't asked for sick leave. She still had three days of vacation left. Should she email Mr. Withers?

Sorry, Mr. Withers, but I have no clue why three days next week are blocked on my work calendar. Hope you can help.

Your scatterbrained employee,

Molly Tipton

No, that wouldn't do. She erased the draft.

Molly shuffled through files on her desk. "Maybe I'll remember over the weekend."

"If it doesn't come to you, ask Tracy on Monday. She manages the company calendar and makes all the travel arrangements. Surely, she'd know," Amy suggested.

"Good idea. Right now, I have to leave. Travis rented a truck. Lissa and Mark are back from their honeymoon, and we're taking my mother's dining room furniture to them."

"That big, beautiful antique set?"

"Laney gave it to her sister. Since Mark and Lissa bought that place in Hyde Park, they have more room than any of us. Gotta run. See you Monday."

On the drive to Lissa's, Molly told Travis about the block on her calendar.

"Do you remember me saying I would be out of town in October?"

"No, can't say I do."

"Any meetings I mentioned?"

"Nope." Travis reached to turn on the radio. He didn't seem all that interested, so Molly dropped the subject.

She asked Lissa over dinner if the dates could have been blocked when they first talked about an October wedding.

"I doubt it, Mom. I didn't have a specific date in mind when I talked about getting married in October."

Molly continued to speculate on what could be happening as they drove home.

Travis turned the radio off. "This is really bothering you, isn't it, Molls?"

"It's just that I can't remember, and that's so unlike me. If I'm supposed to be somewhere and don't go, well, that's just irresponsible. Here, we finally have most of our life kind of moving in the right direction, and I start losing my mind. Doesn't that bother you?"

Travis turned to Molly. "I haven't heard you mention anything for that week because you didn't plan anything that week. I did."

"What do you mean?"

"I mean, I contacted Mr. Withers and planned a little vacation for us."

"Vacation?"

"We need to get away for a few days for some R and R. It's been a big year."

"Travis Tipton, I love you! Where should we go?"

"That's all worked out. Just pack your clothes, and be sure to take a bathing suit. We leave Tuesday after work."

The rest of the weekend, Molly begged him to tell her where they were going. If they were leaving after work, they must be going somewhere close by. Perhaps they were going to a bed and breakfast in the Hocking Hills area in Ohio. It was one of their favorite spots. She imagined sitting in a hot tub with the crisp autumn air around her.

Another possibility was the Smoky Mountains. The mountains were a short drive from Cincinnati. Every time she asked, he would grin and offer her no more clues.

Monday evening, he supervised her packing, saying things like, "You're not taking that, are you?" or "Aren't you going to take a dress in case we go out to eat?"

On Tuesday, Travis drove Molly to her work early before heading to his own office. Both worked through the lunch hour. At three, Travis picked Molly up, and they headed south on I-75, across the river and into Kentucky. *That leaves out Hocking Hills.*

"We'll stop south of Lexington for dinner. That's when I'll tell you. I promise."

The restaurant Travis chose had a two-hour wait.

"I should have made reservations. Now what?"

"I really don't care where we eat. I am just happy to be here with you."

They drove to the next exit to a popular truck stop and ordered Swiss steaks with mashed potatoes. Travis wiped the tabletop with a paper napkin he pulled from the box on the table. "Not the fancy atmosphere I wanted for tonight, but it's better than waiting two hours." He handed Molly a folded piece of paper. "Here. As promised."

Molly unfolded the paper. "Tarpon Springs? But how?"

"We're staying at a bed and breakfast."

Tarpon Springs was one of their favorite spots on Florida's west coast. They had always enjoyed the small Greek community, the deep-sea fishing excursions, and the quiet beaches.

"We'll spend tonight in Chattanooga and get into Tarpon Springs early on Wednesday. If we leave early Sunday morning, and I mean *early*, we can drive straight through and get home in time to go to bed. It gives us three-and-a-half days to soak in everything. Sound okay to you?"

"Better than okay."

Molly dozed off in the car somewhere between Knoxville and Chattanooga, so she was surprised to find they were south of Atlanta when they stopped for the night. It was dark, almost midnight, but already the temperatures were warmer than Ohio.

By six-thirty the next morning, they were on the road looking forward to their special, unexpected vacation. They opted for a drive-thru breakfast but enjoyed a relaxing lunch in a little town in Florida called Land O' Lakes, a half hour from their destination.

"So, what do you want to do first?" Travis asked once they had arrived and settled in their room.

"How about a nice, long walk?"

Holding hands, they ventured up the street of the old town, poking around antique shops and a used bookstore. They each found a novel to read, paid all of a dollar for both, and found a small Greek restaurant for dinner.

The next morning, rested and relaxed, they donned their swimsuits and headed to the beach. Howard Park was a short drive from their bed and breakfast.

Several kite surfers were out on the water, flying through the water and sky, twisting and turning with ease. Molly and Travis stood near the water's edge and watched.

"Would you ever try that?" Molly asked.

"I'm not that daring."

"I don't know. I think you're full of surprises."

The October sun was warm, not hot and glaring like summer. Travis spread their towels on the sand. Within minutes, both were engrossed in their books.

Friday, they wandered in the little shops along the sponge docks and ate at a seafood restaurant at the end of the docks. They located one of the deep sea fishing excursion boats and made a reservation for Saturday morning. It would be their last hurrah.

Thirty-five passengers, mostly tourists, joined them on the boat at six the next morning in hopes of a big catch of grouper, red snapper, or other Gulf fish. Molly and Travis wore windbreakers and stood on the front of the top deck. A pod of dolphins escorted the boat once they had pushed out of the Anclote River into the Gulf. The beautiful creatures swam along the bow of the boat. Every time the boat stopped or slowed, the dolphins would swim deep and resurface somewhere far from the spectators. Molly watched in fascination as the dolphins disappeared, then suddenly jumped out of the water, only to dive back down into the dark unknown. The wind carried with it a spray of salt water.

"Getting cold?" Travis pulled his wife close. "How about a cup of coffee and a sandwich?" He led the way to the boat's galley inside the cabin.

The boat traveled out into the Gulf of Mexico and stopped at a spot deemed perfect for fishing. The sun glistened over the gently rolling saltwater. Now that they were no longer moving, the air was warm and inviting.

Travis baited both his and Molly's hooks. They allowed their lines to sink deep below the water's surface. Molly felt a tug but pulled her line up only to see a clever fish had managed to steal her bait. The day was peaceful. Sitting at the boat's railing, her line leading downward, Molly had time to reflect on all she had learned about herself these past nine months.

Over all, the catch was light for the day. Travis managed to bring in two nice-sized groupers. One of the passengers offered to purchase his catch.

"Not enough to cover expenses, but still fun," he told Molly as he returned from the holding tank in the back of the boat.

Many of the tourists, now warm and anxious to catch the last rays of their vacation, stood by the rails or sat on the benches lining the outer decks for the return trip home. Travis and Molly took their turn on the upper deck as well. The dolphins returned to escort the boat part of the way back. Molly watched them and finally put the last piece of the puzzle of her life in place.

Tired and sunburned, Travis and Molly made their way into the cabin. Two teens sat at a table in one corner of the area playing cards. Molly and Travis chose a bench near a window. Travis rested in the corner of the space, his back against the plywood bench. Molly sat down next to him and pulled her feet up under her on the vinyl cushion. She leaned into Travis, resting her head on his chest. He shifted his arm, pulled her closer, and closed his eyes.

"Travis, I need to talk to you about something."

"To tell me what a wonderful husband I am for bringing you here?"

"I hope to have a lifetime of telling you that. No, this is something . . ." Molly hesitated. " . . . else. It's about God. And me." Molly began by talking about her childhood, about church and her family. Much of what she said was familiar, but today, shared with a new clarity. Like holding her life up to the sun and letting it shine through her, exposing her thoughts and doubts.

To his credit, Travis listened. He listened on the long boat ride back to the docks. He listened, her hand in his as they sat in one of the little cafés drinking coffee and sharing a piece of the sweet baklava. He listened over the strains of Greek music playing at one of the outdoor courtyards as they walked back to their bed and breakfast. He put his arm around her as if to protect her from her uncertainties and fears.

The air conditioner in their room was running, and the cold air assaulted their sunburnt skin. They turned it off and sat on the loveseat in front of the window, wrapped in a blanket.

Travis asked a question here or there. He offered a word of encouragement when Molly's strength seemed to waiver; but for the most part, this was Molly's story.

They talked; they laughed; they cried. And they prayed. They didn't move to turn on the light, even when the shadows of twilight engulfed them. Eventually, the moon crept across the treed lawn and made its way through the blinds covering their window, casting lines of moonlight across their faces.

Spent, Molly and Travis climbed into bed; and the two of them, wrapped in each other's arms, drifted into a peaceful sleep.

Chapter 31

THEY HAD ALREADY DECIDED TO skip the Sunday brunch offered by their hosts in favor of getting on the road early. If traffic and weather played in their favor, they anticipated driving straight through to Cincinnati. Molly slept in the car for the first hour of their travel. She awoke when Travis pulled into a small restaurant for a cup of steaming coffee and hot buttery Cuban bread.

The day grew warm as the sun poured through the windows of the automobile. They stopped again for gas and lunch in Georgia, then continued their journey in quiet reflection for most of the afternoon. Molly would doze off, opening her eyes to see Travis looking at her, a warm, loving smile on his face. Several times, he reached over to touch her arm or hold her hand. No words were needed.

They were near Knoxville when Molly's cell phone rang. Laney.

"Just checking in, Mom."

"Everybody's okay?"

"We're all fine. I knew you were heading back today and was wondering where you were. How was your trip?"

"We're just south of Knoxville. And the trip was perfect." Molly reached over to stroke Travis' arm. "I have a lot to tell you."

"Aren't we lucky to have such great husbands? Lissa and I were talking about wedding vows the other day. You know better, worse, richer, poorer, in sickness, and in health. We all got good guys."

"Look, sweetie, I better get off and help navigate. I love you, Laney."

"You, too, Mom."

Molly smiled and looked at Travis. *Yep, I got one of the good guys.*

Molly called the girls as soon as she and Travis got home. It was a habit instilled by her mother to let everyone know you were home safe and sound.

"Listen, Laney, do you have plans for Friday night? I need to talk to you and your sister about something important."

"We don't have anything scheduled. Mom, you sound serious. Are you okay?"

"Oh sure, honey. Better than okay. It's just something I need to tell you."

"Then why don't I make dinner here?"

"Are you sure?"

"Yep, and I'll see if Lissa can make dessert."

"What should I bring?"

"Dad."

Molly and Travis were the first to arrive. Travis put ice cream in the freezer, while the children rushed to Molly, who held two gift bags, a souvenir for each grandchild.

"Thank you, Grams." Hunter pulled out a blue T-shirt with a dolphin on the front. Ellie pulled out a similar shirt, only pink. Florida was printed in big letters across the top. A few minutes later, once the adult conversation started, the kids retreated to their rooms to play.

"Wow, you two got a lot of sun in a few short days," Laney commented.

"The weather was perfect. Your dad and I had a wonderful time. I can't wait until Lissa gets here, so I can tell you all about it."

"I like the new art piece," Travis said. "Rob said the artist is 'in-house.' Nice."

Molly moved into the living room to view the picture now hanging prominently above the fireplace. It was the picture Ellie had made at church with her handprints forming a tree. The painting was now matted, framed, and featured the words of Isaiah 55:12:

"You will go out in joy and be led forth in peace; the mountains and hills will burst into song before you, and all the trees of the field will clap their hands," Molly read. "I meant to look that up for you."

"Marisol's brother framed it for me. It's my verse," Laney claimed. "In a way, I'm like a tree. A little more mobile, maybe. But not much. I figure if the trees, who can't move as much as I can, clap their hands, I should have a lot of ways to praise God."

Molly didn't move. Tears blurred the picture. Just then Lissa and Mark walked in the front door.

"Look at you! You're both so tan! Here, Laney, I brought a pie." She plopped a frozen pumpkin pie on Laney's lap and turned once more to her mother. Laney looked at the box, reading the directions on the side.

"Isn't the picture great?" Lissa asked her mom.

"Lissa," Laney interrupted. "Did you read these directions? It will take an hour to bake this and two hours to cool. I have rolls we have to bake as soon as the casserole comes out."

The two sisters fussed all the way into the kitchen.

"Definitely back to normal," Travis said.

Laney had made a beef roast covered with potatoes and carrots. She baked a green bean casserole and rolls. Rob's contribution was a beautiful salad with two kinds of lettuce, cherry tomatoes, onions, broccoli, cucumbers, and almonds.

The family laughed and talked all through the dinner hour. Everyone, including Ellie, took part in the cleanup while Lissa's pie finished baking in the oven.

Finally, the men retreated to the living room to watch the football game Rob had recorded on Sunday. They knew the outcome—Cincinnati had beaten Cleveland by a narrow margin—but none had been able to view the game. Travis had been traveling; Rob and Laney had spent the day with friends; and Mark and Lissa had volunteered to help with the youth group at church.

Hunter and Ellie set up a board game on the staircase landing.

Molly sat at the table with her daughters. "So, let's talk a minute."

Lissa frowned. "Sounds serious."

Molly took a deep breath. "Well, first, I guess I need to tell you about the dolphins." Laney and Lissa eyed each other.

"Your dad and I went on a fishing trip in Florida, and I watched these dolphins. They would swim deep below the surface of the water; but every so often, they'd come up and get air." She paused and looked into the living room for a moment before going on.

"This is hard for me, but I need to tell you. I've been like one of those dolphins. I mean, spiritually."

Lissa let out a little laugh. "You got so serious there, I thought you were sick or something."

"Just hear me out," Molly pleaded. "What I am trying to say is that I've been a fake. A fraud. I mean, I knew God existed, but I didn't live like He mattered." She stopped to study her daughters' faces before going on.

"I grew up in a Christian family. I knew all the right words and memorized all the right prayers. But I never really made it my own. Not until now. I've pretended to be a Christian, wearing a mask; but most of the time, I was like one of those dolphins. I've just been holding my breath and swimming in the deep, dark waters of life. I'd surface every once in a while and get a little church or Bible. I think I believed that going to church on Sundays, going through the motions of being a believer, would be enough. I would spend Sunday at church, but then dive back down away from God and try to control everything on my own until the next Sunday. I want to be a bird. I want to live in the air all of the time!" Molly let out a little laugh. "Sounds silly when I say it now."

Laney reached for a hand and squeezed.

Lissa scooted her chair closer and put an arm around Molly's shoulder. "It's okay, Mom."

"I was afraid to tell you two this. I was so afraid you would call me a hypocrite. I just hope you can forgive me."

"Oh, Mom, no, "Laney said. "Actually, I've never felt closer to you. I don't know if you realized it or not, Mom; but even though I gave lip service to God, He wasn't all that real to me either. Not until the accident. I wasn't even a dolphin. I was more of a bottom-feeder. Lissa can tell you. But I've been studying my Bible. It's kind of funny, but it took me becoming paralyzed to become whole."

Molly let out a little laugh. "Actually, your accident is what made me realize I was spiritually paralyzed."

"Mom, did you tell Dad all this?" Lissa asked.

Molly looked at Travis sitting in the living room with his sons-in-law and nodded.

"You didn't start with the dolphin and bird story, did you?" Laney asked.

"Yes." Molly laughed. "But I have to say it sounded a lot better the first time."

"I hope Daddy didn't laugh," Lissa said.

"Actually, he was very sweet. He listened. I think he maybe knew I've been struggling. God was very gracious to me. He gave me a husband who truly is my spiritual leader. I have a feeling God has been gracious to all of us Tipton women."

Epilogue

Beverly, Sarah, and Lissa were the last to leave the women's Bible study group at Laney's. The ice cream cake had been a hit with the dozen or so women who gathered each week at each other's homes to study God's Word and share each other's burdens. Lissa pulled the cellophane wrap over the glass dish and meager leftovers to take home to Mark.

"You want me to help you clean up?" Sarah offered before walking out the door.

"No, but thanks. Mom and I have it covered," Laney smiled. She closed the door and turned to her mother.

"I'll take the kitchen if you straighten up in here," Molly offered.

The two women set about their jobs. Laney's new house was spacious and open. Her kitchen was even better than the first one Evan had designed for her house on Mercedes Avenue. She, Rob, and Evan had talked for hours about lessons learned from living in that first space. A single-story home and the separate family room where the children could play was a better option. In the new floor plan, Laney had access to the entire house like everyone else.

"Do you have work tomorrow?" Molly asked.

"I'm finishing a consulting job for Evan."

"His business is growing, isn't it?"

"Yep, he's fast becoming known as the leader in designing and building homes for people with a variety of handicapping conditions. This one we're working on now is for a quadriplegic, but we just finished a beautiful design for a blind man."

"Lissa told me about that one. Who would have ever thought her mechanical engineering degree would land her a partnership with Evan?"

"Don't let her fool you. She likes the work, but *loves* the flexibility of working from home."

"But that's what makes it so great. Especially since there'll be a little one in a few months."

Molly scraped off the dessert plates and loaded the cups and saucers into the dishwasher. She could hear her daughter moving around in the living area, picking up the papers and pencils left behind by the women. The house still had an open concept to it, but the food preparation area, sink, and dishwasher were nestled in the corner of the kitchen with a wall effectively partitioning that part of the kitchen from the living and dining area.

Laney put a CD into the player. Soon the sounds of one of her favorite Christian artists filled the room. Laney, her voice strong and clear, sang along.

Molly listened. It had been a long journey to bring them here. Words from a nurse in the early morning hours following the accident sounded once more in her ears. "She's breathing on her own. It's a good sign."

Laney continued to sing the words of commitment, praise, and dedication. Molly breathed deep, enjoying the moment.

Suddenly, Laney's voice interrupted Molly's moment of silent devotion. "Mom, come quick! Look—snowflakes!" Laney sat at the front window watching the small flakes as they fell silently to the ground.

The two women moved out onto the front porch. Through the trees, Molly could see the porch light flicker on at her own house. She could hear the voices of her grandchildren as they discovered the early snow.

"Our first snow of the season," Molly said. "And it's only October."

"Not quite the retirement you and Daddy envisioned, is it?"

Molly looked lovingly at her firstborn and answered honestly, "Nope. What is it Beverly always says? 'More than I ever asked for or expected.' Guess she was right. God does know exactly what we need."

The snow fell gently to the ground. Strains of music from the CD poured out the front door into the night air.

Exactly what we need.

Can grace and love be found amongst coffee grounds?

Sonja Parker is about to find out.

Excited to leave her stale life in the big city behind, Sonja takes the money her grandmother left her and purchases Libby's Cuppa Joe, a thriving coffee shop in a small community in Wisconsin's Door County. Sonja may have business sense, but is she ready to face the world on her own?

Sonja soon discovers owning a business requires more than offering a good cup of coffee. She must make major repairs to the building as well as major repairs to her heart. Do the former owners, Libby and Joe hold the answer? As Sonja seeks to make Libby's Cuppa Joe a viable business, can she also find herself and the God she has abandoned?

Libby's Cuppa Joe is a riveting tale of second chances, forgiveness, and not living on borrowed faith.

More Fiction from Ambassador International

For decades, the Reverend Sammy Milton was a force in American politics.

Scott Addison was a product of his time.

On the day Milton died, Addison was assigned to write an in-depth story meant to bury the fundamentalist preacher in vitriol. He expected the piece to be an easy one.

Far from a simple assignment, the story would take him to places he never thought possible.

A Spiral into Marvelous Light
by Michael Gryboski

Ted and Diana Rutherford's dreams of a peaceful retirement go up in flames along with their furniture store one fateful night.

Faced with new challenges, scandalous secrets, and tenuous relationships, Ted and Diana must begin anew. Can they really start over and maintain their hope when the future looks so grim?

Starting Over
by Joanne Wilson Meusburger

For more information about

Rebecca Waters

and

Breathing on her Own
please visit:

www.WatersWords.com
www.facebook.com/RebeccaWatersAuthor
@WatersAuthor
www.goodreads.com/author/show/8087383.Rebecca_Waters

For more information about
AMBASSADOR INTERNATIONAL
please visit:

www.ambassador-international.com
@AmbassadorIntl
www.facebook.com/AmbassadorIntl

*If you enjoyed this book, please consider leaving us a review on
Amazon, Goodreads, or our website.*